# DOLLFACE

## Katherine Rae Fox

*Dedicated to all of my beautiful bookworms, who like to escape reality in the world of the dark and depraved.*

*"Even if it is caused by being broken, I don't desire to be fixed. Not because I enjoy suffering, but because I am Felix Antonov's pretty, broken Dollface-and that is just how he likes me."*

NATALYA LANE

# CONTENTS

# FROM THE AUTHOR

This novella is not for the faint of heart, if you start reading and think it can't get any worse- it can. There are many dark themes. Your mental health is important, please take that into consideration when reading this novella. Love you book family.

# TRIGGER WARNINGS

Physical Abuse

Marking

Religious Cult

Foul Language

Romantic Situations

Suicide; Mentioned

Forced Proximity

Captivity

Torture

Child Abuse; backstory-non detailed

Drugging
Substance abuse

Flogging

Simulated drowning

Stockholm Syndrome

Corpse Medicine

Kissing of a Skull

# DOLLFACE

# CHAPTER 1

*Dollface*

"Alright Nana, I'm boarding the flight." I say into the phone as I step onto the plane.

"Be careful, you hear me? You're our baby girl. Let me know when you land. You know I'll worry myself half to death." Nana barely gets out as pappy takes the phone. Pappy worries too, but he thinks Nana is too worrisome.

"She'll be alright. You're worrying yourself to death, Yelena" Pappy assures his perturbed wife. "Won't you?" He asked me.

"Yes Pappy, I'll be fine. I'm a smart cookie, and I'm very careful. I'll let you know when I'm with Felix. I love you guys." My reassurance comes out as genuine as I can. I adore them both to death, but I'd be lying if I said I wasn't a teensy bit annoyed at how much they fret. I'm a twenty-one year old woman. I'm not a baby anymore.

Well, I should cherish it while I can. Like Nana always says, you never know when the last time you will see or hear from your loved one is.

If it weren't for them, I may not be here today to even leave this little rural town. I could just be sitting in my mom's camper. Freezing my ass off, while her and Tommy hunt like pirates through the sofa for dope money. More like dope change, actually.

Tommy seems alright despite his habit, but I still miss when she was married to Jermaine. He was the coolest of my stepdads. Coolest dad since my real one. He called me his daughter, and still tells people I am. He always believed I was going to get out of this little town and do something big with my life.

Imagine his excitement when he found out I got accepted into Kingston University in the city. That's a big accomplishment for a small town girl like me. I didn't tell Nana and Pappy, but what really drew me to Kingston was the foreign exchange program. I'd always had an interest in studying languages. Hell, I now speak four. Next on my list was Russian.

You could imagine my surprise when I had become aware that it was one of the languages offered at Kingston University, in the little ol' state of North Carolina.

People often ask me why I decided to learn Russian. Well, I already speak fluent English, Spanish, French, and Italian. Not only that, but my mother's family is Russian. That's right, my Nana is Russian, specifically from a small area in Siberia. It is often cold as all hell there, and very secluded. Nana says it's different here. Not more or less preferable, just different.

Pappy was a U.S. soldier traveling the globe when they met. I have never really asked all of the details, but it sounds like a movie. Otherworldly, even. Look at them now. Forty-seven years strong.

Talking to Nana has always made me want to visit one day. I've always been into the whole family history thing. Nana picked up one of the many south-eastern accents after living here with Pappy for so many years. Only when she speaks English, of course. My Pappy found a trucking job in the Carolinas once he retired from the army. Nana says to call her babushka, but I grew up here in the south east, so Nana comes more naturally to me. Babushka was too long for little ol' toddler me, apparently. I have attempted ridding myself of this southern accent for years, but I have only been marginally successful.

Nana and Pappy are great. Sweet and stern. Living with them saved my life as a child. They were far from perfect, but they did the best they could. That best they could, it was great.

It helps them a little that I had made a friend from Siberia in a foreign language exchange group at the university. Although, they still don't trust my Doc yet either.

Felix Antonov and I became friends rather quickly after meeting with the language exchange group online. He's about ten years older than I, and used to be a doctor in Russia. So, I call him Doc as a joke. These days he volunteers for the Cathedral in his area and attends university courses online. Including foreign languages.

We'd been meeting over Talkzone once per week for about three months now. He is so kind, and helpful. Even patient. When I attempted Russian in my painfully American accent, he assured me I didn't sound that bad. I don't believe him one bit, Doc is just too big of a teddy to hurt my feelings.

Felix being the most handsome man I'd ever seen was just a cool bonus. Not that it matters. He'd never shown more than an interest in friendship , other than jokes here and there. He also calls me dollface, and he once claimed I looked like a princess when I smiled. He was just being silly, though. Buttering me up. Probably so I would agree to more study hours, and be more likely to go on this trip.

Did I mention he's also extremely hilarious? I have never laughed more than with Felix. It isn't quite what he says, it's how he says it. That's how I know this is destined to be great! He warned me Siberia was a very cold area, to bring every piece of my warmest clothing imaginable.

I'd packed all I had coming from a coastal state that is warm most of the year until late Autumn. A couple of cute sweaters, a hoodie, pajamas , long socks and some leggings will have to suffice. I'd spent most of my saved cash on the plane tickets, so buying a coat when I had a hoodie was difficult for me to justify.

Besides, it's not like Doc will want to be outside for much in eight degree fahrenheit  weather. He seems immune to the cold, but doubtful he'd subject me to it much.

# CHAPTER 2

## *Dollface*

A s I step off of the plane outside Novosibirsk Tolmachevo Airport, I decide to go inside to make a Talkzone call to Nana and Pappy. Doc isn't supposed to arrive for another fifteen minutes.

I passed sculptures of a man on a horse, a sculpted head, and the most beautiful architecture for an airport. It's making me grow more excited with each moment until I meet Doc face to face. Doc, my charming and hilarious friend Felix. He is allowing me to stay in his home for the duration of my stay.

-

Saying goodbye to Nana and Pappy on Talkzone was very difficult. Their anxieties only grew during my flight to Siberia, and when I told them the temperature, Nana gave me her best *I told you so.* Pappy asked if I'd brought a jacket and some boots. He will definitely have to console Nana after we hang up.

Just when I've run out of things to explore, I spot him. Doc. With his buzzed sandy hair, strong jaw, and those eyes. Wow, those blue eyes are even more captivating in person.

That's not the only thing that is better in person. My mouth drying makes me wet my lips. I nervously nibble at one lower corner with my teeth. Not because I'm feeling uneasy, but because Doc is, well, hot. I hadn't really noticed to what extent before because we don't always use the video function on Talkzone, and honestly my wifi sucks sometimes.

You can imagine my surprise when he strode toward me with his towering six feet and two inch frame. I'm not super short by any means for American standards, but it is enough to still make my five foot six inch gaze have to look up. Doc's nickname should be voted to be altered to Hulk instead. His broad shoulders and incredible arms stretch the soft black cotton fabric of his long sleeved shirt.

Who knew that Felix Antonov is a work of art, much like the tattoos peeking out from the hem of his sleeves and wrapping up his throat to stop at his defined jawline.They're not shitty tattoos either, those cost a pretty penny. More than my car probably in total. My only tattoo is a matching dove on my hip bone, similar to the one my cousin Sofiya has. I just hope he doesn't notice me eyeing him, or blushing. He'd never had this effect on me before, but I'd only previously met him over Talkzone. Who knew he had such good taste in clothes, too.

At the sound of his voice I snap out of it, this is Doc we are talking about here. Not some hot guy from my classes at the university. Not some model, though he could seriously get hired at any company. We are friends, just friends. That is something I'm sure I will have to repeat to myself more that I'd like to admit during my stay.

"How was the flight, Dollface?" Doc asks, assessing me with his baby blue stare. Oh gosh, now I feel underdressed in my white sporty pull-over and black leggings. Feeling suddenly very shy, my cheeks heat and I avert my gaze.

I clear my throat and throw my bag over my shoulder. "Long, but I slept most of it."

Yes, just breathe and react how you normally would. It's' just Doc. Good ol' Doc. Your language exchange friend.

"For you, pretty lady," Doc says, grabbing my attention as we begin to walk side by side.

"A coffee? How very nice of you." I take the coffee from his hand, noticing a little cross tattooed on one of his knuckles. Doc just flashes me one of his warm smiles.

My mind absently wanders into what the cross tattoo is about, not that it matters. My curiosity just always seems to get the better of me. Is he religious? He had never mentioned it when I brought up how religious my Pappy is, and Pappy is a prayer over every meal kind of man.

I was raised in the church. Every Sunday I rode to church with Pappy, and every night I bowed my head before bed to whisper a prayer. Now that I'm an adult, those days have long been gone. I have not stepped into a church since I turned eighteen years old. Not that I have anything against it, it just isn't my speed anymore. I'd say these days I lean much more toward agnosticism, and just try to live my life being the best version of myself I can.

Snapping out of my thoughts, I realize Doc asked me a question. Shit. I need to get my squirrel brain under control.

"Dollface?"

Oh. What a nickname from someone like him.

"Yeah, sorry. " I mutter, then take a sip of my coffee. Mmm. My favorite. Vanilla latte.

"No worries. How do you enjoy Siberia so far?" He asks as we approach what looks to be a black, Aurus Senat car.

Wow, so he also drives a Russian luxury car. Who am I friends with? I keep forgetting that the whole reason I call him Doc is because he was a doctor. Duh, Nat.

"Good so far, but I haven't seen much. Only the airport you know." I smile, and slide into the passenger seat.

Doc starts the vehicle, and turns his head to face me. "I will have to show you around." The playful wink that comes after is nothing short of charming, but it's cold as hell out. I think I'd rather hibernate for the winter.

I snort. "Hard pass, it's cold as a witch's kiss out here. I think exploring once a week is good for now."

"A witch' kiss? Doc's brows knit together.

"It's…a southern thing. Our phrases are interesting to say the least." Embarrassed, I tuck a lock of my brunette waves behind my ear. With my sunny southern girl tan, I stick out like a sore thumb in this place so far. My slang will only make me more obvious.

"I think you are actually so cute." Doc smiles, as he pulls into a driveway.

I don't have time to react to his words before we pull up in front of this cute little cabin. It's beautiful, like out of a farmhouse mag. It actually reminds me a lot of the one my pappy used to take me to when we went skiing in the winter.

"You like?" Asks Doc, as he unlocks the front door to push it open for us. "Women first."

Stepping inside I am in awe. The ceilings are high, there is a gorgeous natural stone fireplace below a large tv on the wall, and the furniture is warm and inviting. It feels like a cozy little home, and well decorated.

"The word like is an understatement, Doc. " My words come out in a breathy whisper as I slip off my boots and take in my surroundings.

"Good, are you hungry? I'm no chef, but I have plenty of food for your stay." He assures me.

"Why thank you, Doc. That is very sweet. Something small will suffice." I reply as I sink into the dark leather of the couch. I sent Nana a quick message on Talkzone saying I have made it to Doc's and I briefly mentioned his nice cabin.

Not very many minutes later Doc sits next to me and hands me a sandwich and some hot tea.

"Thank you, Doc." A small close-lipped smile stretches over my lips.

" It is only a sandwich, Dollface. It was nothing. I need to make a phone call if you do not mind." He returns the same friendly expression and excuses himself to what I am assuming is his bedroom with his cell phone in hand.

Ten minutes have gone by, and Doc is still on the phone. I can't really hear his conversation, only the mumbling of distant voices.

After I'd finished my tea and sandwich, I became quite sleepy. Scratch that, more than sleepy. My eyes and limbs are heavy, and I am having difficulty focusing on my phone screen. It must have been a long flight. Too long. I'm sure Doc won't mind if I drift asleep.

# CHAPTER 3

*Felix*

"When will you give her the Rohypnol?" Asks Father Gurevich, his weathered voice sounding worse over the phone with each call. Father Gurevich may be a priest, but he has been the only family I've known since I was just a boy as well. He is like family to me.

After my mother-after she...

No. I can't think about that right now. All I need to remember is who was there when nobody else was or could be. That someone was Father Gurevich. He took in many young men. Gave us a home. Fed us. Became our new family. Even if his methods were a little questionable. Just like what he wants me to do with my Dollface, and similar to all of his dolls before her.

"I'd just given it to her earlier with her tea. About twenty minutes ago. She should be asleep by now." Sighing, I rub the back of my neck. "

I struggled with the decision this time. Father Gurevich." Truth be told, this recruitment was more difficult than the others. My dollface is the most beautiful of them all. Even her heart and brain are beautiful. I have always had trouble seeing beautiful dolls cracked and shattered. Only a rare few are strong enough to survive Father Gurevich . It got easier over time, I just began viewing them as he always seemed to claim they are. What they are.

My dollface though, I know she has some purity in her soul. I can see it when I look into her grey eyes that gleam silver when she smiles. Father Gurevich will spare her, I can feel it. He will see, like I see. This one we get to keep. We won't have to let her free.

Of course, none of them ever break their physical bonds. Do they? No, not the dolls. Not our pretty little dolls, except for my dollface. My Natalya. Oh,I wish to keep her very much.

Father Gurevich sighs over the line, " Do not tell me you already covet her my boy. We must make sure she is pure, so she does not spread rot upon this community. Now, hang up and go begin your procedures. I will see you both at the church tomorrow. "

"Yes, Father. See you soon."

" Soon. " He replies and hangs up.

Peeking out the door, that's when my suspicions are confirmed. There is my flawless dollface, asleep on my couch. She is even more angelic when she rests.

Lifting my hand I gently brush her hair from her heart shaped face.

" Soon you will be cleansed, doll. Then you can be mine. Isn't that so wonderful? Father Gurevich won't have to take you away like he did the others. " I whisper as I drop my hand and walk away to grab the measuring tape. Father needs to know what size of cage she needs. He has many cages. All of them stained red. Hers will be new

Poor little doll, that will be tough for a sweet woman like her. She can do it, though. I believe in her, because she is mine. My dollface just doesn't know it yet. She is never going back home. Siberia, this is her home. Right here in my cabin. I even got all of her favorite foods and shower products.

My dollface will love me, she will see once it is over. Father Gurevich says when they die, it's because they are full of sin. He says that the sin bleeds out, and if there is too much evil in their blood they don't stop. Then they die. Father Gurevich can only save the pure.

I don't want to hand her to him for one moment, I think as I measure her body. Father will just tell me the flesh of man is weak, and that my dollface has not been proven suitable for marriage in a small, isolated community in the very large Novosibirsk.

Our practices go unnoticed and unbothered due to the large population of the city. We are so overlooked that no one outside of our small area knows about it. Father Gurevich says that will change one day. We can cleanse the outsiders who visit. One country or city at a time.

We have had broken dolls from all over. Nearly all of them give in to the suffering of the flesh and perish. If our lord can be whipped, so can a sinner. That's what the Father claims transcends them from impure to holy. Beatings, lashings, captivity, torturing, and being subjected to the sub zero temperatures are some of his favorite methods. He aims to break the flesh, then the mind. Once the mind is broken, it may be rebuilt. Rebuilt to suit a person of morality.

As a boy, Father Gurevich's practices used to mortify me to my core. I used to wake up screaming, with beads of sweat coating my forehead. Almost as if I had a bad fever.

There was a time when I could still smell the blood, and hear the cries. People would look at me with both hope and horror through the bars of their cages. Their flesh would smell from the crosses freshly branded into the backs of their shoulders.

One broken doll's collar was so tight, it left marks of rubbed raw and broken skin around her slender neck. Her blond hair was wet from the snow. Her lips were chapped and purple from the cold. Her name was Tati. A woman from Moscow. It has always been very rare when Father Gurevich takes a doll from our homeland. Maybe that is why she survived, in his eyes it made Tati Volkov easier to cleanse.

Snapping out of my thoughts, I place a thick comforter over my dollface's body. Poor girl will feel terrible in the morning, as the side effects from the Rohypnol take hold. I will simply tell her she must be getting ill from the drastic change in weather. The same line I have fed countless broken dolls for the Father.

I place a kiss on her forehead, " Goodnight, Dollface."

Then I go to my room and rest for the night, and pray the nightmares stay away. With Natalya, I will not be as strong.

# CHAPTER 4

## *Dollface*

Groaning and squinting my eyes, I notice the sun is still out. Maybe I haven't slept for that long, if it hasn't become dark out yet.

If I haven't slept much; I sure as hell should. Either way, I feel dreadful. Exhaustion has hit me like a train. The only reason my body even attempts to sit up is because my stomach feels nauseated, and I'm parched. It's like that Spongebob meme. Need. Water.

Immediately, I am very aware that it is going to be a bad idea too. I sit up anyway. It just made me feel dizzy, and quite frankly feeling a little disoriented. The only thing that I become aware of is the fleece blanketing my form; other than my sudden illness of course.

Did Doc give me this blanket? Why do I still feel so exhausted? Cat naps usually do it for me. So many questions.

"Doc? " I shout, standing up very slowly in an attempt to control what feels like my sudden onset of vertigo.

When Doc smiles and comes toward me with a plate of pancakes I relax a little.

"For me? Thank you, they look delicious." I take and go sit back down onto the couch. " How long did I sleep for? Must have been a while if you're feeding me again."

"Considering it is now Sunday morning, I would say a very long time. Was it a pleasant sleep?" He asks before practically inhaling his breakfast.

I almost choke on my food. Sunday morning? That means I was out cold all night. So unlike me, I still feel like I could lay back down.

"Holy shit- Doc, I am so sorry. " He was probably so disappointed. My first day here and I slept through it.

"No worries. You are forgiven. Besides, I got the opportunity to speak with Father Gurevich." There's that smile again.

"Father Gurevich?" I ask, finishing up my breakfast. " Is he a priest?" Shit. It's Sunday, now might be the time to mention that I'm not really a church kinda gal.

" Yes. He is so excited to meet you today, Dollface." He says while pulling on a black trench coat and lacing up his boots.

"Right now?." I can only hope I don't sound rude. When it comes to religions I don't judge , nor do I look down upon them. I'm just not sure of what I believe. This will be my first attendance at mass in three years, but Felix seems so excited. I'm sure Father Gurevich is a nice guy . Maybe once won't hurt.

"Why not? Services begin soon. We should get going." Felix chimes, grabbing his keys.

Standing up I play at a warm expression. " Sounds good, let me brush my teeth and grab something warm to wear." I say as I make my way to the closest bathroom, while pulling over my white hoodie. It isn't that I'm not excited, I just didn't expect this to be the first thing we did. My expectations were more like chill, language study, and maybe a bit of seeing the city.

"Sure thing. Father Gurevich is very excited. " He shouts across the room with reassurance in his tone.

Felix's smile doesn't quite reach his eyes. That's the first time I have seen him with that look on his face. Weird. Maybe this Gurevich guy and Felix are close, but I get the feeling it isn't because of his love of attending mass. Felix could have felt pressured, especially if they have known one another a long time.

Same, though. Growing up, my preacher was a friend of the family. He was a really charismatic and genuinely sweet old man. Regardless of me quitting church attendance, my Pappy and I would go fishing with him every Saturday. Maybe it's the same kind of thing with Felix and Mr Gurevich.

" I'm sure he is, especially if he is a friend of yours."

Arriving in front of the Cathedral, my first thought is how over the top enormous it is. The ones back home are impressive, but holy mackerel.
The architecture of these are insanely beautiful and intricate.
A tall building, with the tops shaping into almost a colorful teardrop.

Reluctantly stepping inside, my following of Doc proved the inside even more impressive. High, stained glass windows and ceilings. The light scattering creates casts of otherworldly colors bouncing off of the walls and pews.

*This is how they get ya. Don't fall for it Nat.*

*Okay, so maybe that's dramatic.*

I am in awe, though. It is exquisite in the cathedral.

My fingertips graze along the oak of a pew, lost in being mesmerized. Until I hear a quite matured male voice clear his throat and ask me a question. A question I barely heard because I wasn't being very self aware.

*Of course I'm not. Squirrel brain has me by the tits as soon as I see shiny colors.*

My face quickly heats. I wish I wasn't so easily embarrassed. Anything I do, or any situation I find myself in that is remotely humiliating, weird, or even sexual I flush and want to crawl into a hole or the box of shame. For no less than three business days, nonetheless. It's a curse. Maybe one day I'll grow some lady balls or some self assurance, but today is not that day .

I raise my gaze to the figure in front of me.. This must be Father Gurevich. He's not what I'd imagined. In his 50s, maybe. Roughly the height of an average man, and built like a brick house. Priest collar, the whole holy man shebang.

His voice makes him sound much older, he must have lived a hard life. Or Father Gurevich is secretly addicted to a pack of ciggies a day.

" I'm sorry. What was that?" I whisper, while trying my best not to awkwardly look away. Eye contact isn't my best superpower. Too shy for that really.

Looking around I realize the only person I know on this whole continent is nowhere to be seen. Where's Felix? I followed him in less than ten minutes.

"The Cathedral. It is quite marvelous, isn't it? It has a way of capturing the mind and soul." Father Gurevich gleams. A pearly smile stretched across his mouth. He must have a good dentist.

"It's very gorgeous, Father. Do you happen to know where Felix went?" I'm awkward around new people, but especially alone. Felix has to be close.

"Here! Sorry, I was moving something very large for the good Father. I see you two have met." Felix's voice booms from my left, and I turn my head to see he is holding..rope?

Well that isn't weird at all.  Must have used it as leverage. He did say he was moving large things.

"We said hello. " Reassuring him with a small smile, I pick at my thumbnail. Nasty habit, but some anxious habits take longer to unlearn.

"Told you she was a doll, Father. Is she not?" Felix  as he twinkles approaches us.

"She is quite divine indeed." Not sure why, but the way Father Gurevich says divine makes a shiver run through me. He probably didn't mean it that way, there is a language barrier, after all. He's speaking Russian, and I am still only a beginner.

Except, it wasn't necessarily the words he used, but the annunciation of them. Father Gurevich is likely just some sweet gentleman trying to be complimentary. Here I am being judgmental.

"Thank you, Father Gurevich. Are you Felix's Priest?"

 Why did I ask him that? Of course he is.

Father Gurivich chuckles, likely sensing my nerves. " Something like that."

"Father Gurevich raised me for a lot of my life." Felix admits, now standing to my left.

That is not what I was expecting. Being raised by a Priest must have been interesting. Maybe that's why Felix has never mentioned his parents. He grew up like me. In someone else's home. Could be why I was drawn to him in the first place. I could tell he was broken in some way. Damaged, but optimistic. Definitely explains why today was so important to him. Father Gurevich must not be so bad.

"Well, it's lovely to meet you. Felix was very lucky to have you."

# CHAPTER 5

*Felix*

"**I** need you more than I want to." I whisper as I stroke her light brown waves. My dollface. My dollface fell asleep again after we returned to the cabin and had dinner. I made a hearty stew. Her favorite cold weather food. I accompanied it with crusty bread and wine. Wine laced with Rohypnol. She probably thought she drank too much. It was risky, what I did. My actions need to be cleaned up, and more creative.

She is so pretty it hurts, my lovely little dollface. It is a shame what Father Gurevich has instructed me to do. He doesn't know her like I know her. He thinks she is too much of a sinner to be my wife. All because she is an outsider.

He is wrong about dollface. He will see. Father Gurevich just needs to test her. Just one test. She can prove it to him. Then we can be happy forever. No cleansings. No unlawful restraint. No blood. No tears. Just my Dollface and I. She will understand, I'm sure of it.

Every breath she takes. Every choice she puts into action. Father Gurevich will be watching. He will be watching me too. For now, anyway. What happens if I chose an unclean woman to be my bride? No. No. No. I can't question Father Gurevich. No. He will make it all okay. Yes, he will cleanse her if need be. Mhm. My dollface will be perfect, she is perfect.

"I would love for you to need me and very deeply to want me."My whisper falls from my lips faintly as I tuck her in again.

On the couch my Dollface lays again. Asleep. Pure. Perfect. I need her to need me. I'd love for her to love me. Even when I remove the mask. When I reveal to my Dollface my other truths. Surely in time. Yes, in time.

Now, I must ring Father Gurevich before I go to bed. He won't be very pleased if I don't.

*The phone call*

-

Father Gurevich: "Well hello boy, I had a feeling you would call."

Felix: " I'd not disappoint you."

*Father Gurevich: " You know better. Remember what happened with Kai's girl. Tati Volkov. She still hasn't been relieved of her cleansing."*

Felix: " Yes, Father. Speaking of- what did you think of my Dollface?"

Father Gurevich: " Natalya. Hmmm She is a doll indeed, boy. I have a good feeling about her. Very timid. Will make a great addition to the community so long as she *behaves*."

Felix:" I knew she was perfect. "

Father Gurevich: "That is for me to decipher. "

Felix: "My apologies, Father. What next?"

Father Gurevich: "We begin on Sunday."

-

Phone call ends.

Sunday. Sleep must wait for now. That is not very many days away. Peeking at my Dollface, I marvel at her sleeping form as I make a mental list of my tasks to come. I have to finish building her cage. Use Pyrography stencils to put  dollface onto her collar. It will be magnificent. Blessing  the blade I will use to carve our branding into her unblemished flesh will be the most difficult for me.

She will forgive me, my Nat. My doll. The purest angel on earth. Natalya has always said she thought some scars were cool. That they are tattoos with a story. This makes me smile to myself. Such a smart woman.

Sneaking back into the living quarters I loosely measure her dainty throat column. Twelve inches around, just about. Everything about her is exquisite, she just doesn't know it yet.

All night I work on this collar. Taking my time on every intricate detail is of the utmost importance. Only the best for Natalya. It looks near faultless, much like her stormy grey eyes when she blinks up at me. Seeing it complete draws an emotion from me that I only feel when I think of or look at her. Fuck, it's so addictive. Like Father Gurevich grew to feel for Tati. That's why she wasn't given back.

Surely since he has Tatiana he won't covet my Nat. Right? No, no. Haha. That would be crazy. It would make me crazy, too. Would he kill me like he did Tati's boyfriend? No, no. Father would never. I am his favorite. I know because he calls me. He has me help with all of the dolls. Father Gurevich stopped carving our mark of holiness into my skin sooner than the other guys.

I remember the last day he carved it into me. It was on my back; somewhere among the other four markings. I got one per year until I was eighteen. He claimed I was now rid of the sins of my father and mother. I almost cried tears of happiness and salvation.

Finally, he loved me. Father Gurevich found me worthy of being his sidekick, his friend, and his son. Most importantly, he said our God now forgave me. It was the happiest day of my life. Until I met her.

I have placed the collar on a silken white pillow, in a wooden locked box under my bed. It should be safe there. Safe and unable to be easily stumbled upon. She can't see it before the test. It will be too much. Like it was for Tati and Father Gurevich.

Then she will run away, and I won't be allowed to continue treating my Dollface the way I desire to. Father will be triggered. It will remind him of his Tati. Then he will hurt her. He will hurt my Tati and say she is still riddled with sin. I have witnessed such a thing.

When Tati first stumbled upon the basement of the Cathedral it was an accident. It was too soon. Before Father Gurevich could let it seep out. So instead of it being a cleansing, Tati was restrained and whipped into her compliance. Which was nothing compared to the first one. His very first rotten doll.

Well, she wasn't a doll at all. Was she? She was his Eve. A liar wrapped into an alluring package. A lying, plotting, and impure being. My mother. Mila Antonov. Her maiden name was Babic. She was not from here, only my birth father was. My sperm supplier. Father Gurevich says all females are of deceit, but a few can be shined like a dirty knob to show the purity underneath. That is why we must do what we do. She was an outsider, too. Yes, I remember her well.

Mila Antonov would wail for her boy from the basement of the

Cathedral. From sunup to sun down. One day, she got free from her bindings and ran upstairs. My mother grabbed my shoulders and said we must leave this place. We must leave Father Gurevich and relocate far away. She claimed he was brainwashing us boys, and taking advantage of our impressionable minds. Of our broken homes and spirits. Mother even cried crocodile tears and said the cleansing was abuse. Ha, that it wasn't of God.

Father Gurevich cut off her tongue that night and made us eat a dinner of the boiled protein. He said we must taste the flesh of a sinner. In an attempt to warn us against the blasphemy of Father Gurevich's word. He said liars must not hold the ability to speak, or they will infect others with their illness. Their sin.

Father Gurevich would never be dishonest with us. His family. He did what he should have, and it proved to show us against blasphemy of his name. This will not happen to my Dollface, though. She holds her tongue. Natalya is full of truth and light. That is why she is mine. All mine. If Father Gurevich tried to remove anything to that degree from her I'd-

A knock at the door draws me from my thoughts. I cross my quite small room and open it. My angel has woken from far too long of a Rohypnol- induced sleep. Two nights in a row is cutting it a little too far into the uncomfortable direction, but Father Gurevich wanted to ensure we had time to talk, and I had time to build the cage. Even make her collar. One day Nat won't be my Dollface. She will be my wife. A warrior, like me. A survivor. Worthy of Father Gurevich's blessing.

" F-Felix?" My dollface asks. Poor woman. Rohypnol has some serious likelihood of side effects, and I am seeing a few on her beautiful face. Nat's big and bright eyes house hollow bags below them, and I can tell she is still confused.

I step out of my room and lock it. She barely notices due to the state she is currently in. I would feel guilty if it were not for the excitement shooting through my veins at lightning speed with the thought she may be fully mine soon. Mine the right way. The way that Father will not hunt her and take her for himself as a new edition to his cleansed dolls.

"Is something wrong, Dollface?" Concern as false as Father Gurevich's teeth in my words. I am great at acting, though. I should have gone to Hollywood.

I think I'm getting seriously sick." She curls back onto the couch, using my lap as a pillow. I'm sure she is too out of it to be aware right now, but I don't care. Contact is like a drug from Natalya. Even if it is limited and partially platonic. I know she is just as attracted to me as I am her, but this is not that. She merely needs to be comforted. I can play the caretaker role and miraculously nurse her back to health. My angel would see me as a hero. Yes, that is how I must do this.

My hand moves her hair from her forehead to falsely feel for a temperature.

"Wow. Your head feels like a mini heater, Doll." The lie rolls from my tongue sweetly like candy.

At times I find our lying hypocritical, but Father claims only women must tell the truth. He says men lying for righteousness to protect these Angels is not a sin. It is an act of our Savior, and Father Gurevich is always right.

"Mmmph." She groans and touches her fingertips to her lips.

"Are you thirsty?" I inquire. She probably needs something after sixteen hours.

She mumbles an mhm, and her phone rings. Talkzone. Fuck. Across the screen reads Nanna. I hit decline and brought up the encrypted messaging app. It is one of the only free apps that allows you to message or call anyone, anywhere in the world.

Then I open up their conversation to send a short and sweet

text, trying to mimic Nat's speech and writing style. She is quite affectionate with her Nanna.

Nat: *Hi Nana! Sorry I couldn't answer, I'm getting brunch. I'll call you and Pappy later. Love you!*

Nanna: *Okay, we love ya. Call us later. We have been worrying ourselves to death. Eat something good for me.*

That was easier than I thought it would be. If my Dollface doesn't remember sending the message, I will attribute it to her sudden onset of illness. She has been just so delirious from her fever as of late.

My inner dialogue makes me sound like the most caring psychopath you will ever meet. Maybe it is true, but I do think I genuinely care for my doll. That is why I agreed to do this for her. Nat can remain mine forever this way.

# CHAPTER 6

*Father Gurevich*

"Felix is bringing the lovely Natalya to services on Sunday." Humming gleefully to myself: I straighten my white clerical collar in the reflection of the  vanity mirror.

I stride over to stand in front of the cage, my frustration growing at my darling's silence. Firmly gripping the bars, my face inches closer until my nose nearly makes contact with the chilly metal.

"Tati, darling? Did. You. Hear. ME?" This time there had better be some acknowledgment when I speak.

Tati has been thoroughly trained and broken in. Like a little house pet. She knows when to eat, shit, and surely when to speak.

My angel gets this way at times, petulant. Childishly sulky. Pitifully fretful, even. It is the sin trying to worm its way back into her brain. The disobedience, which took weeks to chip away at.

"Tatiana, you will get a lashing. Speak.  I did not break my Priesthood vows in keeping you, for you to be as silent as the light fixture on the ceiling."

I yank the keys from the hook they rot on most days, and unlock my pet's cage.

Once I step inside and sit on my haunches to face her, my darling decides to let out a whimper. She hugs her knees to her chest, and presses her back against the opposite cage bars.

My darling dolly hardly allows her big chocolate eyes to connect with mine. When she does, it is ever so fleeting. Too quick, even.

My doll's puppy eyes are what made me sin when I'd seen her. I had felt something people often feel for attractive people. She pushed me to break my oath. To sin, and I had loathed the whore for it. Just like I had attempted to do with the other dolls, I tried to fix her. Tried desperately to make her less physically appealing, and less tempting. More pure. I will be no Adam. Swindled for a mere apple by the likes of a beautiful woman.

There was only one thing to do. The only way to keep Tati as my forever doll was to rid her of all of the temptation and sin. To cast it out of her like medication does to an illness. She needed to become broken, to be whole again. Whole and perfect.

I had known my darling dolly was different from the dolls before her. She had proven it to me, too. When she survived. When the cold didn't end her life that week I chained her outdoors on a cross. When the holes from the nailing of her palms did not bleed out. Yes, my darling doll is a survivor.

Now, she is all mine. Just like Natayla will belong to one of my boys. Felix. I'd taught him well. His lashings and lessons were not wasted. He didn't end up like my first son. Vlad. Vlad could not withstand his cleansings. I found him hanging in the Cathedral in front of the podium.

At first, my instinct was to shed a tear. Later that night it was to cut sinner into his cold skin with his own blade. The one I had gifted him for when he found a doll to save.

Everywhere on his body it read sinner, in jagged carvings. I'd used that night as a lesson. I had demanded the other sons participate in their brother's after- death cleansing for the sin he had committed.

My hand had held onto their trembling ones as they wailed. Every tear they shed for his mutilation was a lashing. Felix even vomited like it was the most gruesome thing they'd observed. Spare the rod, spoil the sons.

My other guys had not seen the worst of it until many years later. The first incident was when I cut off a woman's tongue and fed it to them. I still chuckle at their faces when they tasted it. That night was out right righteous for my soul. Especially the impure pieces. It was scrumptious, all of the thousand yard stares and hollow blinks. It served as quite the lesson, didn't it?

"Stand up, darling doll. You may need to eat again. As you know, we have meals together in the Cathedral." I press a kiss to her forehead, and she doesn't grimace this time.

Her once warm eyes remain cast downward. My darling dolly is closer to as broken as needed to be rebuilt. The sooner she reciprocates and follows along, the more I will believe Tati is closer to purified enough for public showing.

At this moment she is still quite infectable by outsiders. By sinners, even after all of this time. I have faith , though. Faith tells me she will be a work of art and proof of a successful cleansing.

Tati stands on shaky legs. They were once toned stems that seemed to reach her navel. Now they resembled battered stilts. Her now hollowed cheekbones made her face appear modelesque rather than ghoulish. She is perfection personified. Even when fasting regularly.

That is why she must have regular cleansings. To satiate my need for her, and starve it away by seeing her as a weak rabbit. Not the fiery fox that I'd first had to tame.

"Good. Now follow me, darling. You have got a lovely salmon up the stairs, and into the kitchen."

My mouth presses to her temple as I lead her to her first meal in days. Tati follows me without protest this time, too.
At least, until she surprises me with speaking her first full sentence in months. It has me halting mid-step.

"F-father-will you  make Felix harm the girl?" Her voice is small,cautious.

Over my shoulder I answer her truthfully. "Natalya will only be harmed as much as she resists, and for good reason. To be with my son she must be cleansed.  You know this, darling doll."

"Will y-you promise me s-something, Father?" Her voice trembled, and was dry.

"What could you possibly need from me, Tati?" My question is rhetorical as we finally reach the kitchen table and take our respective places.

" Promise me you won't make her suffer." Tati requests, while finally locking eyes with me. I can not remember how long it'd been since she had done so willfully.

Oh, how endearing. As well as maddening. Does my darling doll still not see that this is for their benefit? Would they rather their sins or their previous lives corrupt their souls?

I grit my teeth as my hand clenches around the fork I am holding. Suddenly, my feelings are as though Tatiana has forgotten her place here in this Cathedral. There will be some regret for that later.
Right now she is shameless, and an utter disappointment.

What a damned pity. Look at her now, inciting thoughts of rage in me. I will not allow her to corrupt my emotions. She will not taint my soul. This may be more than a lashing.

After my darling doll eats, she will wash the dishes and kneel. She will disrobe, to feel the humiliation as I do after falsely assuming she had made progress over the years. It makes my stomach utterly ill. The little wench.

Then, I will give her lashings until I have cleansed and prayed away the fury and embarrassment in my mind. Yes, that will do it. Lashings until it breaks her tender flesh. It will be excruciatingly delightful to see her bleed out the defiance from the open wounds.

# CHAPTER 7

*Dollface*

Sitting on the oak of the porch banister, I sip my tea and stare blurrily out into the vast space of forest. Snow blankets the ground, and peppers the treetops. Not a bird or animal in sight.

My outfit of choice being jeans and a long-sleeved henley, I'm surprised I could dress myself this morning, much less pick out clothing.

Thankfully Doc had some hot tea and pastries ready. He must have really had to look out for me these past few days. I have been feeling so out of sorts that I only recall flashes. Bits and pieces.

Felix was a saint, from what I remember. He would cover me with a warm, thick comforter. He's opt to bring me soups and tons of water. He had even called my Nana for me.

Felix was such a gentleman and I could not be more grateful. This morning, though, he said we were attending mass. Then, we were to have dinner with Father Gurevich at the Cathedral.

I don't have the energy, nor desire to do such a thing. The guilt would eat at me though that he had done so much for me lately, and I couldn't do anything for him.

That is why despite my inner protests, I will go with him. We haven't gotten to study languages or hang out much since I arrived.

The door behind me creaks open and out steps the man himself, and damn. He is dressed impeccably, I feel grubby as hell now. Clearing my throat I mutter a hello.

"Hello, dollface. Are you ready?" There's that smile again.

"Ready as I'll ever be. You sure you want me to tag along?" I motion toward my messy bun and outfit. He just chuckles.

"Yes, doll. I want you with me. Today is quite important." His reassurance helps a little, I guess. He just looks so good, and he would be standing next to someone who looks like they have never slept in their lives.

" Okay, Let's go then." I hop off the banister and follow him to his ridiculously nice car.

-

◆ ◆ ◆

The Cathedral doesn't have many attendees today. It appears to be just Felix, Father Gurevich himself, some woman with gorgeous midnight curls and myself. Maybe people aren't very religious in this area, or maybe it's a special occasion.

No, that's silly. If it were, Felix would have mentioned it. Right? Yeah, I'm overthinking it.

Approaching Father Gurevich and the other woman, the Priest's face slowly spreads into a huge, toothy grin. The woman hasn't so much as glanced my way. Weird. Who is she?

I must have made an impression last time with Father

Gurevich, though. His arms outstretched offering me a hug. I'm not really a hugger, but I oblige. I'm afraid to be rude to anybody here. I would hate to cause problems for Felix.

Something doesn't seem right, though. Today is Sunday, there should be mass. The cathedral should be full.

"Father Gurevich, where is everyone? It's Sunday." I question during our quick embrace.

His smile is meant to be friendly, I'm sure of it. It just appears strange instead.

"The weather hardly permits anyone to attend this time of year. Besides, this is all we need. Just perfect, actually."

Felix and Father Gurevich share an amiable look, and Felix clears his throat. Wonder what that was about.

"Dollface, let me introduce you to someone. This is Tati. She lives at the cathedral." Suggests Felix, as he places an arm around me.

Earlier I didn't get a good look at the woman standing in front of me, but now that I do the first thing I notice is how pretty she is. Her round teddy-bear brown eyes, long blonde hair , and how tall she is. She could seriously have been a model in her younger days. She reminds me of Monica Bellucci, if she bleached her hair. They're not twins, but they appear as though they can be sisters.

The second thing I take in is how frail she looks. At first glance I thought it may have been age, but at closer inspection I noticed how slim she is. I'm not body shaming, but this isn't natural. My observation comes purely from a place of concern, not judgment. Her cheekbones aren't just defined, they're slightly hollowed. Her striking eyes aren't just noticeable, they're encased in sleepy bags underneath. Her hands are quite elegant, but quite calloused at the fingers and palms. Even in severe distress she is charming in a way.

They said her name was Tati. That's eastern european sounding, I wonder if she too is from Siberia. Since that is where we are after all. Her features, though, lend to elsewhere. I wonder how she knows Felix.

"Hello, Tati. Lovely to meet you." I present my hand in offer of a proper handshake.

At first , I didn't think she was going to shake my hand. It takes her a moment, after blinking at it.

Then, Tati smiles warmly at me and takes my hand in hers.

"It is a pleasure." She mutters, and I see something that utterly confuses me. Pain flashes across her face momentarily, a mist glazing her eyes. Did I hurt her when I shook her hand? I've always been told I have a firm, confident grip. As taught by my Pappy when he taught me about shaking hands, and job interviews.

No, that's not it. Tati drops her gaze, gives me her back and excuses herself.

"Did I do something? " I infer genuinely, flicking my gaze up to meet Felix's .

"No, Dollface. You didn't. Tati- she's had a difficult few years. She will be okay. " He assures me, but I'm not so sure.

He must see it in my face, because he wraps his muscled arms around me and says, " I promise, Dollface.", and my heart explodes.

I'd had a harmless little crush on Felix before I saw his captivating blue eyes in person. Far before I'd seen his stature, corded muscles, and all of these tattoos. Especially, before his intoxicating scent has filled my nostrils. He smells so good.

The embarace is over far too soon before Felix walks me to our respective seats in the very front row, as Father Gurevich smiles and begins the sermon.

◆ ◆ ◆

Once it's over, I remember why I don't attend these things. No judgment to those who do, but that got kind of weird.

At one point, Father Gurevich blessed us in Russian and said he was going to begin the purification of our souls. From that point on, I was squirming inside at nearly every word.

He even bowed his head, after placing his thumb in the "blood of the pure", aka none other than fake symbolic blood. Like the kind they use on movie sets, I'm sure. He even thumbed a cross on our foreheads. I'd never desired bolting from a pew faster, but I stayed for Felix.

He didn't seem to mind the batshit practice, nor was he surprised. I can only hope he is merely appeasing Father Gurevich. Felix is great, but I'm not sure of how long I can play pretend in this department. Which, I don't like to do anyhow.

I mean, I believe in God. I just don't do all of this. This isn't even typical of a Catholicism mass. I'm fairly certain what we just participated in was a Father Gurevich special. One I seriously don't desire to be a part of again anytime soon.

"I hope you like Sarma. Remember that we have dinner plans with Father Gurevich and Tati." Felix speaks softly, his breath caressing my ear and the skin just below it.

"What's Sarma?" When it comes to food, I'm not picky. Especially since I've enjoyed the art of cooking alongside my Nanna since childhood. I just don't really have much of a sweet tooth, I'm more of a savory kind of gal.

"Sarma is a pretty common food in Serbia. It reminds me of a variation of your cabbage rolls. It consists of minced meat, pickled cabbage, tomato sauce and sauerkraut stuffed into cabbage leaves. Sometimes the minced meat is replaced by smoked bacon or fish.

They say it's a dish from the Ottoman Empire. Greece or Turkey specifically. Not sure how it became a popular dish here, though." Felix explains.

Some people might not be down, but I'm not super picky. My Nana made a version of cabbage rolls growing up. So for me , it might not be so different. Apart from the sauerkraut.

"Sounds promising." I remark, as I allow Felix to take my hand in his, which surprises me. After which, he leads  me behind Father Gurevich into a lower portion of the Cathedral.  Does Felix have a little crush too? This could be normal for him, I think.  I just sure hope it isn't. Could he feel my palm getting clammy, and hear my breath hitch?

We reach the kitchen. Which-a kitchen in a Cathedral? First time I've ever seen it. I'm obsessed, though. It is surprisingly modern, yet cozy. It has a similar style to Felix's cabin .

A large cornerstone fireplace is off to the side of the room, where an oak table with four chairs is centered. The sandy-colored stone design continues up that wall, and the other walls the same beautiful oak as the table. The light fixture is a bronze chandelier, with 6 teardrop light bulbs.

The stove, refrigerator, and sink are separated by a small door you walk through. There are barely any words to describe how incredible this place looks. The Father must live here full time.

Felix pulls my chair out for me. Demanding myself to hide the flush it brings to my face, I avoid his piercing gaze. I can't allow myself to be the first one to show interest. Not because of some weird ideation of waiting for the man to make the first move, I'm just incredibly shy. Plus, I really don't want to risk making anything awkward between us. Especially after I've just arrived.

Felix takes the seat next to me, Father Gurevich sits across from him, and Tati takes the seat across from mine.Her eyes remained downcast, fixated on her plate for most of the meal. Then, she grabs some wine. She even pours Father Gurevich a glass, which surprises me for some reason.

"Natalya, how long do you plan to stay in Serbia?" Father Gurevich asks, raising a brow.

"Well, I'd planned on staying long enough to fluently learn Russian from Doc over here, and maybe see the city a bit. Or, as long as Felix will have me I suppose. I don't want to overstay my welcome the first time around." I answer, lifting the glass of wine to my lips.

As the first sip hits my tongue my senses are surprised with the fruitiness. It has notes of oak, is strong and surprisingly smooth. Likely one of the better wines I'd had lately. Not that I do a lot of sampling.

"This wine is great." I smile, looking up to my right at Doc. Although, lately it has felt very odd to call him that silly nickname. I have been referring to him as Felix more since my arrival. Doc was the knowledgeable and wholesome best friend-Felix is something else entirely.

"Glad you think it is so good. It is called *Tri Morave*. Remind me to snag a bottle from Tatiana and Father Gurevich. " He winks and I feel an immediate pang. I know it should make me smile, like usual. Though, the knowledge that he couldn't possibly want more from this chips away at me.It isn't what I'm here for, so I can't allow myself to be too hung up on the notion that there could ever be something more.

"Also, in reference to your stay with me- I may just keep you." Felix jokes.

My head tilts upward in an attempt to return his smile, but I can't seem to focus on his face. My vision is blurred, and I feel a little dizzy. Am I still sick?

"Tati and I sure wouldn't mind having you around when we see Felix. It'll be refreshing to have another woman in the Cathedral every now and then."

My eyes darted to a very pleased looking Father Gurevich, but Felix must notice something is wrong. He places a palm on my shoulder and turns in his chair to face me.

"Nat-are you okay? You don't look very well right now." Asks Felix, the  concern in his voice causing my anxiety to skyrocket.

"Y-yeah, I just think I'm still -" The words won't leave my lips, and I place the wine glass on the table. I'm no longer able to keep it in my grip. My muscles feel relaxed, weak. Is this the Flu? Could be.

"Calm down, you're okay. Don't fight it, Dollface." Felix says. I think it was Felix,anyway. He's fully facing me now, gently holding me up by my shoulders in my chair, with his hands placed on my shoulders. His eyes filled with- something I can't place.

What did he say? To not fight. Not fight what?
That's when I realized, I'm not ill. I've trusted the wrong friend, and he's betrayed me.

"Why?" Is all I can force out of my trembling, numb mouth as I feel the slickness of tears wet my cheeks.

"I'm sorry, but I had to. You'll see, Dollface."

That's the last thing I hear before it all goes black.

# CHAPTER 8

*Felix*

N atalya slumps over in my hold, finally succumbing once again to the Rohypnol . My dollface looked so hurt by me. So betrayed. Fuck, this is not how I wanted this to go .

I knew Father Gurevich and I were going to begin the cleansing soon, I just didn't know it'd be tonight. It should have been obvious with his dinner invite and all.

A pain spreads through my chest. I wanted more time with my precious Dollface. More time before we broke her. I wanted to study with her, eat her favorite foods. The desire to simply watch a film of her choosing had danced across my mind. I craved the luxury to have made her mine before she potentially hated me. This could realistically go either way , and this is the first time I've allowed myself to see that.

"Oh Dollface, please don't hate me when this is over." I whisper and pick her up.

"Follow me, boy." Demands Father Gurevich, his mask slipping as he begins to take charge. I hope he doesn't forget that this is MY doll, and she is flawless. He will not remain in charge here when it pertains to Natalya.

Tatiana is already sobbing, as she paces slowly behind us.

Once we reach the basement, I lay her gently onto the bed in her cage. I'd finally finished its intricate design. I'd decorated it with her favorite flowers, yellow roses. And placed a new journal, with a pencil on the floor next to her mattress.

Twisting my torso to the side, I'd picked up the box encasing Natalya's collar. I finished that last night, too. It was metal, bronze. The collar had letters reading Dollface across the front, and locked with a key around the back. Like the sun, it shone bright under the light. That's what Natalya had reminded me of, the sun. So bright, and beautiful. Full of life. Now look at what I've done.

No, I can't think that way. Father Gurevich says it must be this way. I can't question him. I shouldn't. This is the only way to keep my Dollface forever.

Across the room, Tati's sobs grow louder than I'd ever heard them. Tati never cries, she accepts her place here. With Father Gurevich. So, why is she crying tonight?

I turn and approach her cage. She's already been locked in for the night-or week. Who knows anymore. I haven't been in this room since - nevermind.

"Tati-What's the matter?" I questioned. Something about tonight must have seriously gotten to her.

"Felix.." She whispers between sobs, "Do you care for her, this Natalya?"

"Yes, very much." I whisper back to Tati, my hands wrapped around the bars of cold metal.

The pity in her eyes is something I have never seen from Tati, and I have witnessed her withstand some brutal things.

Tati's eyes darted back and forth between mine a moment, almost searching for something. Whatever she finds gives her great pity.

"I believe you, Felix." She assures, cupping one side of my face through the bars with her slender hand. "But…if you love her, you will find a way to end this."

Those words are like a slap to the face. How dare she. I'm doing this because I love Natalya. I'm doing this so Father Gurevich allows me to keep her. He won't take her if she's been cleansed. Doesn't Tati understand?

Rage bubbles to the surface, but I quickly bury it deep inside. If Father Gurevich sees this weakness he will make me take a lashing.

"You know nothing of what you speak." I bite out, and push away from the bars of Tatiana's cage. My dollface won't be so ungrateful.

Giving her my back, I threw over my shoulder, "You're wrong, Tati. This is the only way to show I care."

"Felix- there is no love in here." Tati throws out, as I make my way across the room near Natalya's cage.

Father Gurevich stands on the outside, admiring the sleeping beauty. Not with interest, he has his precious Dolly Tati for that. I'd say it's more so him being pleased with my work.

"You're doing the right thing, my boy." Father Gurevich reassures me, placing a withered palm onto my shoulder.

Sometimes I'm not so sure where Natalya is concerned. I wish I could be normal. My wildest dreams are for a long future with my Dollface, but my confidence decreases with each betrayal toward her. Even for the sake of her soul. As Father Gurevich would say, *We are all sinners. Sin must be purified from us, then we may be accepted. Especially our dolls. They are riddled with temptation. A temptation man cannot afford.*

"What is it?" Questions Father Gurevich.

I blink my gaze to his, my mind lost in everything my pretty little dollface must endure. Starting tomorrow. I had never really questioned it until now, but I just can't fathom her understanding. Anxiety tickles my pulse, but I quickly squash it.

"Nothing, Father." Clearing my throat, my watching eyes drift back to my sleeping beauty.

"You're not questioning my methods, are you?" He demands, his voice remaining direct and deceptively calm. I know the truth. What it means to question him. To doubt his methods.

"No, Father. Never." I swallow, barely meeting his unique heterochromia eyes.

His grip on my shoulder tightens, and his voice becomes momentarily lethal.

"Good. You know better." He reminds me. As if I needed the reminder.

Before passing through the doors to leave, I take one last look for the night of my Dollface. She looks so at peace in her sleep, even in the midst of my betrayal. I don't wish to leave her, even for a night, but there are things I need to prepare before the morning.

"Soon, Dollface." I mumble, before turning away and making my way out of the Cathedral for the night.

Father Gurevich remains in the basement with the cages, likely to have a word with Tati about her behavior this evening. For which I'd like to stick around. Not because I'm a sadist, but I'm curious. She didn't want me to leave Natalya here.

It's not that I don't have first hand experience as to why, but this is the only way. It's the way Father Gurevich raised me, after all.

We began in our own cages, my brothers and I. After some time, we graduated to a shared room, then our own rooms.

The lashings went from distributed by Father Gurevich daily, to self-flagellation during prayers most often. Unless we disobeyed of course, unless we sinned.

*-Flashback; Felix,ten years ago-*

'Our Father,
*Who art in Heaven..."my voice trembles, the cries to my left nearly drowning out our words. We can't stop the prayer, we can never stop.*

*THWACK!*

*"Hallowed be thy name,
The kingdom come.."*

*THWACK!*

*"Thy will be done, on Earth as it is in Heaven.."*

*THWACK! THWACK!*

*The sound of whip cracking is nearly shattering my concentration. The wailing to my left has stopped, but the lashings have not. I suspect my brother has reached his point of shattering. Like me.*

*The sounds of footsteps shuffling to the right, making the hairs on my neck stick up, and my pulse quickens.*

*No, no not today. I haven't forgotten one prayer yet. My cleansing is complete. Father said so himself.*

*"Felix, do you know why it is now your turn to receive this lashing?"*

"N-no Father G-Gurevich." *My answer is meek and fragmented.*

*He bends down to mutter in my ear, making me swallow in fear.*

*"I saw the weakness in you, as your brother received his lashings. You didn't put the word first in your mind, instead the well being of man. You may be cleansed, but do not forget your place, boy. Now, start again."*

*THWACK!*

-Flashback over-

Placing my old crucifix into the bag, I glance down at my trembling hands. My breaths quickened, and I down a glass of water I'd placed on the table beside my duffle.

It really awoke something that I thought was long dead inside of my mind, after being in the Cathedral basement. Father Gurevich hasn't needed me to come down there in years. All of our meetings are elsewhere, or in the Cathedral's kitchen.

The feel of the bars. The smell of the wood. Everything about the damn place triggered me. Which terrifies the hell out of me. What if I'm not strong enough to do this? What if I can't be the one to cleanse my Dollface? Then he will have to, Father Gurevich.

No. That can not happen. I will not allow that. He doesn't feel for Natalya like I do. He won't stop, until she breaks again and again. It has to be me. I have to be her bad guy. For now, anyway.

I pull my phone out and scroll through endless photos of my Dollface. My smile can't help but to escape. Everything about her is perfect. Her hair. Her eyes. That little smile she gives. Even how ridiculous it is that she flushes and blooms like a rose so easily at small things.

My lips press briefly to the screen, and I tell her how I will be by her side in the morning.

# CHAPTER 9

*Dollface*

Waking up, I try to stretch out my limbs. Only, when I do, I fail because my limbs feel so weak.

Upon shifting from my side to my back, my throat feels ever so slightly constricted. *What the hell?*

Panic starts to creep into my chest, and my eyes want to fly open. The only thing they can successfully do is squint open ever so slowly.

*Why do I feel like hell right now?*

My fingertips inch up to touch my neck, and I notice there is something around it. Something metal. Upon further inspection I trace letters with my fingertips.

*Is this a collar? Is there a collar around my neck?*

Now I'm really starting to freak out, so I sit up. What I see makes me come to a full body halt.

*I'm in a cage. A fucking cage.* This has to be a nightmare. This can't be real. Except, as I try to recall the events from last night my eyes widen at the realization that I was drugged last night. By the Priest, his-whatever Tatiana is, and potentially Felix.

No, Felix wouldn't do that. Not my sweet, funny Doc. Oh my god, what if they hurt him? My eyes dart around the room, until they land on another cage. There's somebody in it.

"Felix!" I scream. " Felix, is that you?"

The figure moves closer, but it's not Felix's handsome face that I see. It's Tatiana.

*What the actual hell is going on here?*

"Tati-Tatiana, where's Felix?" I demand through my cage bars, and gripping at my collar.

"He should return soon, they will want to begin early."

*What did she mean by that-about beginning early?*

"Tatiana, talk to me. Tell me what's going to happen."My voice began to strain from the yelling.

"The cleansing." Tatiana says quietly, approaching her own cage's bars to face me.

"What the hell is the cleansing? Cleansing what, Tatiana?! And why do we have to be in these cages?" My demands run my voice ragged, making my throat begin to ache. I need to save my voice, but there are a lot of things that I need answers to right now.

Turning, I find a bottle of water next to the mattress I have been given. I pick up the bottle and gulp down about half, not knowing when I will be afforded more. Then I darted my gaze back to Tatiana. How long has she been here? Then I realized, that's why she was so upset upon our arrival to the Cathedral this evening. She knew.

Oh, God. Did Father Gurevich hurt Felix? Where is his cage? So many questions are firing off in my brain a mile a minute. Though, I have a sickness deep in my stomach telling me I will know soon enough.

"There is no escape, you know. Once one of them decides to keep you, that you belong to them; they do this." Tatiana warns, her voice void of any emotion. Not because she lacks it, but because she has exhausted all that is left of herself for the day.

"What do you mean they do this? What is all of this, Tati?" My words are becoming more unintelligible with each one I speak. Tati said they, not he. They.

"Tati, did Felix bring me here, to stay with him, for this cleansing?" Tears threaten to fall but I won't allow them. Not again, not yet. Being weak won't help me much right now. I need to get my shit together for the time being. The betrayal of my language exchange partner, and playful best friend, doing this to me nearly shatters me. Nearly, because I refuse to allow it. I'm my Pappy's granddaughter, I'm a fighter. I'm a Lane, damnit. Lane's do not give up. I will find a way out of this, and I'll take Tati with me.

Felix is in a complicated situation, devochka." She mumbles, her big brown eyes filled with agony.

"What do you mean?" I question, sitting cross-legged on my mattress.

"Father Gurevich has brainwashed this into him since he was a boy. I should know, I was there for many of those years. Felix is nothing but a sweet, broken boy fulfilling the wishes of the man who raised him. The same man who terrorized him, and made him participate in despicable things. All under the guise of purity, religion, and affection. Felix is unwell, sweet girl." Tatiana's eyes no longer hold mine, as a muscle ticks in her jaw.

"That's-that's horrible, Tati. Felix never told me. He never mentioned his childhood to me. He had seemed so…pleasant. That means he too needs help, though." My heart warms at the memory of the first time I'd ever studied language with Felix, my silly Doc. Then it fades as quickly as it came.

"He cares for you, Natalya. Very much. He believes this is how you show such emotion." Tatiana responds, giving me her back. "Get some rest, devochka. You will need your strength."

Laying back on my mattress, my mind drifts to Doc. My Felix. This is terrifying, and heartbreaking. If Tati is right about his feelings for me, then maybe I can convince him to let me go. To remove this damn collar, and unlock my cage. If only he'd not been broken. Then he would know that I had fallen for him, too. Now, his actions have changed things. Permanently. Though, it does make me very aware that I could be susceptible to Stockholm Syndrome. Which, now that I think about it, may be a true motivation of Father Gurevich's side of the practice.

What does this cleansing entail? We are in a Cathedral, and it is the sick idea of a wildly disturbed Priest. A religious cleansing, then? One Felix believes is necessary to keep me or show love. What the hell has this Gurevich guy taught Felix? Tati said Felix was tortured, made to do and see horrible things. Did Father Gurevich lock him in a cage, too? Oh, gosh. I feel sick at the thought of a little Felix living with a monster like him. Now look. He's making my Doc, my Felix, a monster.

Tatiana says I should rest, but I'm not too certain I can. Not only that, but I also doubt whether I should even close my eyes in this place. Who knows what the hell they have planned for me.

"Tati?" I question, my eyes burning from me forcing them to remain open.

"You should be sleeping, Natalya." Her soft accent reminded me of Nana's, just a little younger of a voice.

"I'm finding it difficult to." I admit, releasing a deep sigh, and shifting to lay on my side.

"If you do not, you will regret it." She reprimands. Tati doesn't sound rude when she does this, only motherly. I suspect that is her goal. She has been through this before. I'm just not sure how to dull the anxiety long enough to squeeze my eyes shut. Let alone for hours.

"I don't plan to be here long. Tatiana. And when I leave, I want you to come with me." My admission sounds less confident aloud than in my head.

Tati laughs. She laughs. It lacks the joy of laughter, though. This is something else. Maybe she has finally gone insane, too. Just like Felix apparently.

Felix, who apparently even in this situation can't seem to leave my thoughts. It's just, yesterday we held hands. Today, he is one of my captors. It's difficult to go zero to one hundred where Felix is concerned, but hey, They say the Devil was an angel first. He must have hurt for so long, but I wonder if he didn't get a little bit addicted. Father Gurevich sure did, and I wonder what he says when he kneels to pray. Especially with the knowledge that he has human beings in cages in the Cathedral's basement.

One day, when he kneels down to pray, Father Gurevich will be bowing to me. He will be lucky if he doesn't have to be harmed in our escape. I'm not a murderer, but I won't allow myself to wither here like a plucked little rose petal either. Everybody has a Jekyll and Hyde, I'm discovering. Thus far, I'm the only one that doesn't wear a disguise. They've got to hide their true faces, I think, as my eyes get sleepy.

As much as I'd benefit from being awake, my body is still suffering from small side effects of whatever drug they gave me. It's making me tired, weak. Those are the two things that I cannot afford to do in the morning.     I will make it out of this alive, but I won't get it by depriving myself of basic needs right now. Tati is right, the rest will be good for me. Not that I have a choice, as I finally drift into a deep slumber.

# CHAPTER 10

*Felix*

U pon entering the Cathedral's basement, the first thing I do is go check on my Dollface. Sleeping proved difficult for myself last night, as the guilt began to consume me from the depths of my being. I don't know why I feel it, I hadn't before. Maybe because it wasn't a reality yet, and I had always understood why it must be done. I hadn't locked her in a cage yet, though. Hadn't yet collared her. Hadn't yet left her in the Cathedral basement. Without me.

Noticing she seems to be sleeping, I glance back at the door. Father Gurevich isn't here yet. I unlock my pretty little doll's cage and step inside.

She's perfect this way, in a few hours she won't be in such a state. I watch the rise and fall of her chest, convincing myself this is still a faultless plan. That it is surely the right thing. Father Gurevich wouldn't say the cleansing was necessary if it wasn't. Her soul needs it, right? If I love her, I'll care for her soul.

After walking over to the metal surgical slab, I unzip my bag and empty the contents. Arranging them in order of use, I release a heavy sigh. Before me is a flogger, my special blade that Father Gurevich gifted me many years ago, a crucifix, wine to symbolize

51

the blood of Christ, and various medical supplies. My nickname isn't Doc for nothing. Before assisting Father Gurevich he did allow me to go to medical school. I even had my own practice briefly. Before he realized he could use a Doctor's specialties, that is.

I remember that day vividly, the day Father Gurevich acquired my assistance in this very basement of the Cathedral. It was for Tati. She had just tried to make an escape again, after confiding with a couple who attended a mass here.

Father Gurevich caught wind of this, and set forth her punishment. She was stripped of all clothing, for humiliation. A symbol of his own in that moment. Tatiana was then taken to a nearby forest in the dead of winter and tied to a tree, subject to the falling temperatures and elements that'd betray someone who had nothing to help them. The snow blanketed every inch of Earth for miles. Ice clung to the branches of surrounding trees.

Every day for one week, Gurevich would return to Tati. He would only allow her to accept him gripping her jaw and pouring wine down her throat, and he gave her daily bread. He claimed she could only ingest the body and the blood, that everytime she disobeyed it was Satan pulling her away from him. It was by sheer madness that she had survived.

When Father Gurevich had finally felt mercy and cut her bindings to release her from the tree, she was like something from a horror film. Tati's body had scrapes and cuts from bucking against the tree. Her frail body had rope burns and bruising from being restrained. Tati's skin was so white, it was almost blue. Her toes were nearly frost bitten. I'd had to remove one, actually. I did it in the most sterile, medically accurate way you could perform a procedure such as that in a basement.

When I'd first entered the Cathedral basement that night, Tatiana was curled up next to the fireplace. She was curled in Father Gurevich's lap. He was petting her thick, curly mane and whispering a prayer. It was the first time I'd witnessed him torn from his own actions, he sure did not show such remorse when he'd punished my brothers and I.

That is precisely why I must be the one in charge of my Dollface's cleansing. She will be made pure for me, and I can ensure Father Gurevich is merely on the sidelines. I could not bear to watch him be the one to hurt her. Nobody can hurt what is mine, except for me. Yes, that's what Natayla is. She is mine, and will be in every sense of the word very soon.

It is how Father Gurevich was allowed to break his vows and force Tati to wed him, after her cleansing. He'd claimed God accepted her now, and that this was the only way.

The sound of steps outside of the door drew me from my thoughts. Father Gurevich. He had finally arrived, and began neatly laying out his tools for proper cleansings directly across from mine.

"Hello, Felix."Chimes Father Gurevich. There is far too much pep in his step for my liking."Exciting day isn't it?"

"Excited for this step to be complete, truthfully."I hesitate to answer, but the truth comes out of my mouth anyway.

"Cheer up, boy. Today is the day you begin your sweet little Doll's cleansing, and ensure your lovely Natalya can be one of us. Forever."

He's right. I don't like it, but this must be done if she would ever have a chance here.

Father Gurevich blessed two buckets of water that were sitting side by side in the middle of the room, while faint shuffling stirred from Natalya's cage.

*I'm so sorry, Angel.*

There will be but only one purpose for those buckets of water, their baptisms. If they don't comply we must grab them and force them under. Even if they fight, buck, and scream. Just like Tati's cleansing. I'm sure she is only here to act as a demonstration, unless she is being punished for something. She likely challenged Father Gurevich's decision to do this to Natalya. Tati's cleansing was complete years ago, and she rarely challenges Gurevich. If ever. I'd only guessed it because of the seed of doubt she planted in my head. She's exactly why the guilt slithered in and started feasting on me like crows pecking at the flesh of a corpse.

Now that I've realized it was her doing, the excitement is beginning to flood my being again. It tastes so sweet, too. Knowing once my Dollface is cleansed, saved. Once she is purified, she is mine. All mine.

Natalya was awake now, her almost silver gaze reflecting more of a pewter. The air was thick with tension. The candles flickered, emitting an ominous glow around us. The new excitement mingled with the thrill tapped into my most primitive emotions.

"Hello, Dollface." I grin wolfishly down at her, before lowering to my haunches in front of her cage. "How is my angel today?"

"I didn't want to believe it." She whispers, making me frown. Why isn't she excited? Oh-right. My Dollface just doesn't understand yet. She will soon. Like Tati did eventually for Gurevich.

"Believe what, Nat? That I'd do what I could to keep you?" My lips curl up in the corner, as I stick my fingers through the bars to brush her beautiful hair from over her eye. I tucked it behind her ear, making her bottom lip quiver.

"If you wanted to keep me, Doc, you'd have let me out of this cage by now. I didn't want to believe it, you know? That you were involved in this-this sick shit." She spits, the venom in her voice causing me to wince a little. It hurts that she is angry, angry enough to stop calling me Felix. I'm Doc again for now, but once she is one of us, she will be happy again. I just know it. She needs to stop cursing, though. If Father Gurevich hears her, he might cut her tongue. Might even burn the tip of it with a lighter. That's what he did to my brother, Dimitri.

"Shhh, little doll. No need for cursing. You don't know what you're saying." Hoping my words hit their mark, I rise to my feet and unlock her cage to lead her to the center of the room.

When I attempt to walk her out of the cage, emphasis on attempt, she bites me. Not a warning bite, either. She gets in there, her teeth sinking into the flesh of my hand. Skin breaks, and blood trickles from the holes. When I look at my Dollface, with my blood filling the spaces between her teeth, I can't help but feel warm. In her defense, she was just in a cage. It's so she can't run away. Can't Natayla see how much I desire to keep her? This had the opposite effect of what she was going for, I'm sure. Now, I just feel like a part of myself is with her. I feel like she sealed her belonging to me, and I just want more. I wonder if I'll feel that way when I make her bleed, too. Father Gurevich has already gifted me with the pleasure of cleansing her. I can break every part of her, for the sake of her soul. Then, I can piece her back together. The feeling is intoxicating to me.

"Are you ready to begin, son?" Father Gurevich inquires, now that Tati is kneeling before him, next to a Natayla that is kneeling before me.

"Yes." My voice in awe at the anticipation. Not because I want to harm my precious Dollface, no. Still not that, although that blood idea did send a rush through me momentarily. It's that soon this will be over, and I will have Natalya to myself.

"Let's begin." He instructs me, then we give the command for each of our pretty, sinful dolls to bow their heads.
Tati listens immediately, she'd been through this before. She knows the consequences of disobedience inside and out. Especially when it pertains to improving for our creator.

My Dollface however, is glaring tear-filled daggers at me. Her soft, feminine chin lifted in defiance and strength. Tsk, tsk, tsk, doll. You're showing your unwillingness to obey. How can she be obedient to our Almighty, if she can't for me? I don't want to have to do this next part, but I must. Especially as Father Gurevich is eyeing me carefully, to  ensure I don't fail. That is something I cannot afford to do, or he will do this for me.

So I wrench Nat's chin upward in what I'm sure is a rough grip, and growl, "Bow your head, Doll."

To my utter dismay, she still holds my gaze. Refusing to do as I ask, and I don't ever remember her being combative. It must end now.

I twist her hair in my hand and force her head to face downward. The action wretches a pained yelp from her, one I also cannot allow myself to acknowledge.

"Bow. Your. Head. Natalya." My voice was firm, and clipped. My grip on her hair does not waver until she caves and bows her head.

"Good girl." I praised her, then Father Gurevich and I instructed the next tasks for phase one.

*The cleansing; Phase One:*

1. *Bow your heads.*
2. *Repeat The Our Father after us.*
3. *Practice it  in unison.*
4. *Say the Our Father, heads bowed.*

*Rules:*
1. *If you disobey, disrobe. If you embarrass us or our Lord, we will humiliate you. Until you respect the word.*
2. *If you refuse to say the prayer, one flogging for each refusal.*
3. *If you forget the Our Father, you will be flogged until you repeat it*

*correctly.*
*4. If you fail, You will get a mark of the blade. A crucifix, carved into the flesh to remind you of your place.*

Tatiana repeats the Our Father, head bowed, giving Father Gurevich a sense of pride and approval. She's been previously cleansed, though.

My Natalya, well, that began entirely differently. She's been demanding I let her go. As if I could ever let her go. Everytime she attempted to stand, I forced her by her shoulders back to the floor. Her knees are a little scuffed and bruised, but that comes with the lesson. I'd had many bruises when I'd done this.

# CHAPTER 11

## *Dollface*

**W**hat kind of mindfuck is this? Making us kneel and say Our Father? If any of these people think they could hold me captive in a cage, and then demand anything from me they should think again.

Tati over there is acting like Father Gurevich's broken puppet. Well, Natalya Lane is nobody's toy. Gone is the sweet southern girl. I'm sweet as pie, some would say, but this is too damn far. It's irredeemable. It shocks me to my core that the handsome, giving man I thought was my friend is my captor. Do I feel bad for Fe- I mean Doc's upbringing? Absolutely, It for sure has a lot to do with how his brain works right now. That doesn't mean I feel bad enough to bend at his will, in front of his evil as all hell Father Gurevich. The twisted fuck.

"Natalya! Did you hear me? I SAID to repeat an Our Father. If you don't, you leave me no choice, Doll." Felix warns.

"Do your worst." My teeth are gritting so hard that it hurts my jaw.

"You heard her, boy. You know the rules." Father Guevich reminds Felix, handing him a flogger.

My eyes grow wide in disbelief. Are they-are they planning to use that thing on me, all because I won't repeat their little prayer? I knew I was in deep shit, but I was blissfully ignorant to what level.

"Disrobe." Felix orders, his eyes flashing with annoyance. He can't seem to grasp my resistance.

A laugh escapes my lips, not from true humour, but I really am in awe of his audacity. " Are you going to use that on me if I don't, Doc?" I ask.

'Yes." He replies, raising an unamused brow. What happened to that guy from before all of this? Well, I suppose he never existed. Did he?

"I will absolutely not remove any clothing for anyone on this EARTH who has delirious notions that all of this serves a purpose. You are the definition of insane if you thought otherwise."

His eyes briefly flash with pain, then he releases a deep sigh, and momentarily places the flogger on the table to pick up his blade.

"What's that for, Doc?" I ask, trying my best to hide the fear in my voice.

"It's Felix. You're through with calling me Doc. I didn't mind before, but now that you'll be a part of my life indefinitely you will refer to me as Felix." He grits, pacing toward me, with the blade flicked out of his knife. Father Gurevich shifts over here as well.

"I'm sorry, Dollface. You just can't keep breaking the rules of the cleansing." Felix stands behind me, as Father Gurevich holds my shoulders firmly rooted to the spot.

"Wait-Felix. What are you doing with that thing? Look, I'm sorry just don't ki-" My words are cut off as Felix cuts off my clothing from the back. My breath shakes as I suck in air, preparing myself. Nothing else comes. My clothing slides off around me. Shock morphs into embarrassment, as I keep my watery eyes steadily locked onto the floor. My hands scramble to grab the fabric, before it's knocked away.

I'm unsure of why I thought they'd think rationally about my choice to not listen. I just had to push back. I'm not beginning to go weak, but Pick your battles, as Nana would say. Poor Nana, probably worried sick.

"If you don't start following my boy's directions, it will be myself in charge of the cleansing. Felix has taken a liking to you, but I for one cannot stand petulant behavior. Fix it, for we are only trying to make you suitable under the eyes of our creator." Asserts Father Gurevich, before he winks and gets up to lean against the table. The menacing, sadistic fuck.

"The next time I order you to disrobe, you will. Now is a good time to start listening, Dollface. I believe in you, it'd hurt me greatly if this fails." Felix's voice is harsh, but I can hear another emotion underneath. As if this isn't the norm for him. Maybe it isn't. Maybe Father Bloodlust usually takes the reins, and now it's Felix's turn. Father Gurevich's warning rings in my ears.

*If you don't start following my boy's directions, it will be myself in charge of the cleansing*

He means every word of that, and I have a haunted feeling that if the psycho Priest was in charge; he could care less about giving me warnings.

With self preservation in mind, I bow my head and begin to repeat the Our Father. The anxiety, and with my flight or fight kicking in, it makes it taxing as hell to focus on the words. They seem to just be leaving my lips in a robotic, automated way. So much so, that when Felix instructs me to say the Our Father from memory, I draw a blank. Almost as if I hadn't just repeated it for an hour. It's like how my classwork would be easy, but during tests my anxiety would choke me up, and everything would suddenly go blank. I don't do well under mental pressure, but now is not the time to cave to my previous ailments.

Relaxing myself with steady breaths, I search the depths of my mind and begin the Our Father.

*Our Father who art in heaven,*
*Hallowed be thy name.*
*Thy kingdom come.*
*Thy will be one,*
*On earth as it is in heaven.*

*Give us-*

Fuck! I draw a blank. Give us, what? Give us-Give us our? My pulse quickens. It's day one and I have forgotten the basis of what we had spent over an hour of learning.

"Give us, what?" Questioned Father Gurevich.

I don't dare lift my head, I'm afraid of what I might see if I did. What is the punishment for forgetting? They said there were rules. Felix acted as though he'd feel displeasure in having to enforce them on me.

That's when the handsome devil's boots come into my field of vision. Felix has stepped closer, then he lets out a sardonic laugh. As if he is exhausted with me today. Lifting my gaze ever so slightly, I notice he's picked up the flogger, making my blood run cold.

"F-Felix, what do you plan to do with that?" My voice breaks, as I attempt to keep my tone steady, confident.

*Don't show them fear.*

"Phase one of the cleansing, Rule number three is if you forget the Our Father you will be flogged until you repeat it correctly. The purpose lies in giving you motivation for remembering." Father Gurevich answers for him, as Felix now moves behind me.

The sounding crack of the flogger reverberates through the basement, as a searing pain shoots through my bare back. A strained cry wretches through me, as I attempt to dig my nails into the flooring. I dig so hard they ache, and feel as though they'll either ip or pop from my fingers.

"Start over, Dollface. Say the Our Father, from the beginning. The line you were looking for was- Give us this day our daily bread." Felix reminds me. Ih he thinks I will bow after that, he is seriously ill.

"Fuck. You." I spit, not willing to give either of them the satisfaction. Turning my head to face Tati, I see her head is bowed. She is still as a possum playing dead, the only sign that a human is in there, is the tear that escapes down her cheek.

"Tati", I addressed her, "What the hell is wrong with you? Listen to me, if we fight them off together-"

*Thwack!*

The new crack against my skin makes me swallow my words. If they think for one second that this means I will suddenly obey, they can think again. No, no they haven't broken me yet. What's a little pain?
My laugh sounds demented, no humor in it at all. I meet the eyes of Father Gurevich, fixing me with a smirk. It makes my blood boil.

"If you think you're going to have an easy time with me, you're fucking wrong. I might bend, but no way in hell will I break, nor will I be a part of your little cult." I spit at his feet.

Father Gurevich snarls at me, gripping my hair at the scalp and tilting my head up. "You dare defy the acceptance of God?", his spit flying out with the harshness of his words.

"There is no God in this basement.", my laugh is maniacal. Unhinged. What do you know, this pushes him further. Just how I knew it would.

"The Whip." He demands from Felix, shuffling to stand behind me as well.

"Father, please. You said it could be me to do this. Her punishments could be from me, you assured me." The panic in Felix's tone is palpable, making the hairs on the back of my neck rise. I couldn't show it, though. They can't win. Father Gurevich cannot be afforded a feeling of triumph. Not yet, not until the time is right. Until I can use it to my advantage to get the hell out of here.

Felix, as disturbed as he is, seems to hold a soft spot for me. That's when I see the clearest strategy. To what lengths will he go to ensure Father Gurevich doesn't go too far? I would never normally condone playing with someone's feelings, but in this case I may just have to rely on them to aid in my escape. I could get closer to Felix, play the part as his "Dollface", a name that now makes my skin crawl. Then, I turn them against one another, or I convince him to allow me to escape. I need to begin now, if I want to go home anytime soon, and I need to be shamelessly convincing.

"I-i'm sorry Felix, you're right. I need to learn the *Our Father.* I'll start over, and I'll take my punishment." My spine straightens, and my jaw clenches as I prepare myself for the lashings I'd earned.

Father Gurevich's impatient voice rumbles," Last chance, It's day one. If you can't cleanse her of her clear demonic nature, son, then I will ." He moves away to command his Tati, seeming pleased with my sudden submission to Felix.

"Good girl, Dollface. I knew you would come around." I hear the relief in his voice, then the taint of regret as he utters, "A punishment is still required from before." If he has so much regret, why doesn't he put an end to this absurdity?

*Maybe because it's all he knows, Tati did say Father Gurevich raised him.*

No, I must not allow myself to feel guilt-ridden. He's an adult, he knows what he is doing. Felix will not be victimized. Maybe he waa one at a point in time, but now he is a monster. A very confusing one.

Shaking away my thoughts, and slipping back into reality, I begin to repeat the Our Father again. I receive a lash from Felix after each line. The skin of my back blazing with the feeling of inferno with each break of skin. Skin that must have broken, as I can feel the trickle of what I'd assume would be my blood. The tears rush to my eyes, but I don't allow them to fall. I won't give Gurevich any gratification.

We can't be the first, Tati and I. There has to have been a lot of carnage in this room . Every other room of the Cathedral is stunning, immaculate. Not here. It seems to go back in time a bit. It's cleaned regularly, but the stains that must have at one point seeped deep into some places. One can only assume how much blood spill causes those. Whoever it belonged to , lost their lives. That I am confident in.

Nonetheless, I take my lashings without complaint. Apart from a few involuntary whimpers, I eventually completed the Our Father correctly. After two tries, That is twenty-six floggings. There are thirteen lines in the Our Father, including the Amen at the end. Doubled, that gave me twenty-six. My body is stiff, and I can hardly move without wincing. The desire to cry in agony is palpable, but I can't allow it.

After Tati and I successfully repeat the Our Father, it is apparently now for us to intake our daily body and blood. Bread for the body, which will be our only meal for the first week. Wine for the blood, which will be our only drink. Felix and Father Gurevich claim fasting is important in phase one of the cleansing.

When Felix approaches me with the wine, I uplift my head.

Preparing to drink, I reach out my hand, and Felix orders them to remain by my side. Confusion fills me, until he places a gentle grasp on my jaw. Understanding hits me, and I part my lips, not wanting wine to be spilled down my gown if I don't comply.

Seeming satisfied with my cooperation, Felix's blue eyes find mine and soften. He brushes my bottom lip with his thumb, and places the glass of wine to my lips. He whispers for me to drink it all, even though it seems like quite a lot at once. Then, he breaks freshly baked bread with Father Gurevich, and feeds me some, like I'm his pet. I'm not, but the kindness radiating off of him , with his close proximity makes my pulse thunder with anticipation.

Just as quickly as it came about, it vanished with a tangible quickness. Felix stands back to his full, towering height, then a new mask falls over his handsome face. Like whatever will happen next is serious. Then, I realized why.

"You did so good today, Dollface. Even with a rocky beginning, there is just one last task of the day. Then you may rest." Felix murmurs, almost to himself.

"What's the last-", my words are cut off as each of the buckets of holy water and placed in front of Tati and I. I don't know exactly how they intend to make use of it, but I know without a doubt it's going to be really shitty.

Felix grips the back of my head. Father Gurevich grabs Tati's as both men begin chanting a sacrament prayer. After the first few lines leave Felix's mouth, my head is abruptly shoved into the bucket's water. He holds it there, despite my thrashing, as he repeats line after line. Panic crawls into my mind, after it senses the hypoxia. Disorientation fighting for my thoughts, but I won't succumb. It can't be much longer. Prayers can't be that lengthy, even for baptismal reasons.

At just about the moment my lungs beg to stop fighting, my head is pulled out of the water. My gaps and intakes of breath echo, bouncing off of the walls. That's as close to drowning as I've gotten since the sixth grade, when Saoirse Dornan had to pull me from a pool on a field trip. Ever since I'd sworn off swimming. I guess this wasn't, but the mimicked feeling of the water overtaking you took my mind right back to all of those years ago. Only, there was no Saoirse Dornan, and there was no swimming pool.

The next time I become aware of my surroundings I'm being cradled into brawny arms, against a strong chest. We are walking somewhere, but not anywhere far. I blink, only to peer upward into eyes so blue, they remind me of the sea near the Amalfi Coast. Felix.

Just then I'm no longer in his embrace, and I've been placed back onto the mattress in my cage. He tucks me in, and keeps me company until Father Gurevich calls him away. Then, I drift to sleep.

# CHAPTER 12

*Felix*

I t's officially been one week since my Dollface first began her cleansing. One week in her cage. Seven days of reciting prayers. Seven days of being away from where she belongs, with me. At my cabin, now our cabin.

Every evening after her cleansing, I'd clean Natayla up. I'd care for her, wrap her up, and carry her to her cage. Most times, she'd be depleted, and would immediately fall asleep. A couple of times, though, she'd be awake enough for me to hold. To dry her wet hair, and plait it how she had always liked.

At first, she would struggle against me. Her newfound dislike of me was a slap in the face, but now, it seems those are the moments in the day she looked most forward to.

Although I'd supposed that if you have nothing but religious lessons ,and lashings; you'd enjoy anyone's company. If it meant you no longer had to endure any more suffering, you'd look forward to it.

Everytime I really take in her beauty, I wonder something. How can such an innocent woman have such lethal beauty? I'm falling in love, but I can't make a thing of it. She wouldn't accept it right now, but she would soon . My perfect Dollface. My angel. My light.

As today is the seventh day, we begin phase two of the cleansing. We move on from the baptismal near drownings, and reciting prayers for countless hours. We move on from praying until our mouths are dry, and we are tipsy from the wine. The hunger pangs no longer have to be ignored, but arguably this phase is both better and worse.

Continuing to watch Natayla sleep, I twirl my blade in my fingers. As of late, this is one of my favorite ways to see my Dollface. It might sound creepy, but the reasoning isn't. I think so, anyway. These are the only times he is at peace, and not under severe scrutiny and duress.

Everytime I inspect her form, I find something else to admire. At times it's her hair.  Other times, it's her shapely form. A great combination of slim and curvy. I try not to stare too much at her sinful body, as lust can quickly go too far. She's a dark little goddess, being risen into a messenger of faith, from pain. She's nerdy and sweet, but she's mine. Her mind is a beautiful thing as well, my Natayla, but if you're lucky you'll catch glimpses of its inner workings

That'll all be remedied once she's officially mine. My patience with this process is just thinning. Natalya was meant to be mine, regardless of religion. I can't say that to Father Gurevich, though. He'd have my head and feast on my corpse in front of her.

"Will you really mark her, like the Father marked you? Like he marked me?" Tati's voice is soft, genuine curiosity in her tone.

"If I must." I answer softly, my eyes never breaking away from Natalya.

"She will be very hurt by you for that." Tati murmurs.

Tati is probably right, but that doesn't mean the denial doesn't drive rage through me.

"Oh yeah-how do you know?" I challenge. .

"It sure hurt me when it happened." She answers, her voice laced in pain. Not physical pain, but something much deeper.

"Nat isn't' like you", I explain, "and I'm not Gurevich."

"AH.", she breathes, "you think you are the only one who has loved."

That I did NOT expect. I had always thought Gurevich and Tati were mortal enemies. Had she loved him, is that what she was implying? No, ha, that is absurd. She was a working girl, a brothel worker when Father   Gurevich saved her. He had a distaste for Tatiana from the beginning, especially due to her job. He saw her as the ultimate project, filled with many sins. That's why he'd always been so nasty to her, despite having immaculate control with biting his tongue in the name of religion.

I snorted, "Maybe you loved him, but mine and Natalya's isn't unrequited."

Silence stretches over the room. When I think Tati has given up on talking to me, she says, " It wasn't my love that was unrequited. " Then the room falls back into stillness. It's pure bliss, I don't want anything to distract me from watching my Dollface.

"Father, how did you meet Tatiana?" I question carefully, the man is unpredictable after all.

His motions momentarily still. He clears his throat before inquiring, "Why do you ask, boy?"

"No reason, I just didn't think you had ever told me, Father." I try to keep my voice even, in an attempt to not give away just how curious I am.

"Has that wench said something? She hasn't gotten into your head, has she Felix?" He approaches me, standing far too close for my liking.

Something flickers in his eyes. Fury? No, I'd seen him angry countless times. Was he-worried? What would he need to worry about? Tati was a brothel girl, and he is a Priest. Come to think of it, how would a Priest have met a brothel worker? Maybe she had attended mass, in hopes of being cleansed. With the idea of being saved.

Schooling my expression, I answered him with a casual, "No, having Nat here made me curious. My apologies. Father Gurevich."

He eyes me warily, before slipping his blade beneath his Riassa and nodding his head toward the cages.

Let phase two begin.

# CHAPTER 13

## *Dollface*

I wake to Felix unlocking my cage, and handing me what looks like breakfast. Are we permitted to eat more than bread now? May we drink more than wine?

Pancakes sit in front of me now, with two sunny-side up eggs and some fruit. Felix also hands me a bottle of water. Thank goodness, I thought the lack of hydration was going to be what did me in eventually. No matter how strong a spirit, basic needs can strip you of your lifeforce quickly.

The only thing that kept me sane, was the small glimpses of compassion and humanity Felix had afforded me each evening after our prayers. That might be fantastic and all, but us having a real breakfast might not be so good of a sign. I won't hold my breath, because this can only mean that phase one is complete. I wouldn't know how many days have passed, due to the lack of phones and calendars around here. It's like the goal is to strip us down to bare bones, make us feral or broken, and rebuild us into their purified little fantasy people.

Not only that, but I am a thousand percent positive I'm in very real danger of developing Stockholm Syndrome for Felix. It doesn't do me any justice that I had real interest in him before this, and I'm in denial. He has a crooked smile and striking eyes. But his soul, it is  more than morally grey. It's such a trip to be in this situation, and then every evening be awarded scraps of the old Felix. That is precisely why as I play my cards, they better be played correctly. I  have to keep myself distanced mentally. There is no room to forget how fucked this whole thing is.

I've only stopped fighting, in an attempt to gain his good graces. To make him fall deeper, harder. Enough for Felix's guard to be down. Enough for him to want to save me, even if I double cross him to get out of this hellhole.

"Thank you, Felix. For breakfast." I award him with the most genuine smile I can conjure up.

He smiles back at me, not suspecting a thing. "No problem, Doll. Phase one is over now, today we will begin phase two. Which means you can eat real food."

"How exciting." I replied, giving him my arm so he can lock it with his and lead me to my demise for the day.

As he had for the past week, Felix leads me to the center of the basement room. There isn't anything special about it, but that just happens to be where the tables, supplies , and an altar is.

He instructs me to kneel. Only, Tati isn't kneeling today. I know she has had what they refer to as a proper cleansing before, but they had been making her participate right along with me. This time, she is still in her cage.

Felix must catch the flicker of confusion across my face, because he asks, "What's wrong, Doll?'

"Nothing, just surprised to be kneeling alone." I begrudgingly admit.

This time Father Gurevich answers me. "Yes well, my pet needs caging for the day. We can't have her trying to intervene at any point this round."

"Yes, this week will be a bit of a struggle. Now, enough chitter chatter. Let us begin." Father Gurevich's gleam unnerves me, and I shift my gaze to Felix.

"Natalya, we will now enter phase two of your cleansing. Here are the rules.." Says Felix, as he reviews each one with me.

*The Cleansing; Phase Two*

1. *Kneel*
2. *Say the Hail Mary*
3. *Confess your sins*
4. *Bloodletting ; sans leeches. The idea is having the ability, with God's assistance, to bleed out illness. Your sin is your illness.*

*Rules:*

1. *If you refuse to kneel, your head will be held into the holy water until you stop thrashing. No death. Only simulation.*
2. *If you fail to say, or forget the Hail Mary, you will be marked with our blades in place of the flogger. One cross curving per failure.*
3. *If you lie, we choose between tongue microcuts, and burning*
4. *You will be Marked with a blade, if you refuse-we crucify you. Without death, every evening, for the week, and you can bleed the sin of defiance from the holes in your palms. We may even get the leeches for your wounds, if you show you may need it.*

After hearing the tasks and rules for the week, I now see why they felt the need to leave Tati contained. Is this what she and Felix had gone through all of those years ago? Father Gurevich becomes more vile to me as the days pass.

Felix knew this was my future, and had the audacity to bring me a pancake piece offering? Yeah, fuck that guy. He's smoking something if he thinks for one minute that I will be sliced up like I just got a back rub from Edward Scissors-for-fingers.

"Do you understand the rules, Natalya?" Asked Felix. It's obvious he is eager to begin. I'm just not sure if it is to get it over with, or if he just likes it. He seems to have both sides fighting to come out and play at any given moment. It's given me serious whiplash.

"Yes."I answered, my head still bowing. Fighting before I have Felix or Tati on my side will only earn me holes in my hands right now. Or a bloodied back, No thanks. I'd just have to feign subservience a little bit longer.  Phase two's requirements have forced me to the realization that I must somehow expedite my escape.

"You'll do great, Dollface. Remember the rules." assured Felix, as he places a forefinger until my chin and tips my head up to face him. Only to softly place his lips to my cheek.

Rising up tall, he commands, " Bow your heads, and repeat the Hail Mary."
-

◆ ◆ ◆

Today the stakes were much higher. Today, I've paid more attention,and I received no punishments yet. There is only one thing left, the bleeding. It's like how a very long time ago people once believed a physician could use bloodletting to treat or prevent illness. Only, this is in reference to bloodletting out my sin. Father Gurevich seems to see his view of defiance as an illness, one that needs to be cured in humanity. Especially women, it seems.

"You've done well, Natalya." Felix praises, his eyes shining with pride. "Now is time for the bloodletting."

Felix fetches his glorified human carver, and asks Father Gurevich for assistance in keeping me still.

"There is only one cross, Dollface. Two lines." Assures Felix, as if two or four cuts on my skin makes a difference to me.

Instead of cowering, I sit tall and confidently, but my thoughts don't match actions. The only thing that matters here is how I respond outwardly. If I had acted out or shown weakness, the consequences would be severe. The eyes of Father Gurevich on my skin set fire to my expertly contained rage, the anticipation hanging in the air. The tension around me felt like a noose that grew tighter within each millisecond. It was not just the bloodletting I feared, but what my initial reaction to Felix's blade might actually be. My emotions have to remain schooled to near perfection. Almost tauntingly so. But that isn't all that plagued my mind, it was the realization of my own errors. The weight of my choices pressed down on my chest, as I barely held my breath. I thought I could just temporarily move to a new continent, with only having met Doc, my Felix, through language studies online. It was a futile attempt at an escape from my mundane, yet broken, life. Now the gravity it all was reigning down unyieldingly, and there was not yet anywhere to hide from it.

When the first cut of Felix's knife graced my skin, a throbbing ache sliced through the back of my shoulder, but the physical pain isn't what registered most. What really began to chip away at my resolve, was this is when I figured out I was in love with Felix. Him doing this to me picked at me slowly, but there was still a part of me that resisted. A piece that wanted to lose my shit and push back against these fucking lunatics.

As the cross line of the cut was made, I took in a deep breath, and felt the tender sting. But instead of feeling shattered and broken , there was an inkling of something else-determination. When I escaped this place, I would no longer just be Natalya Lane. I'd be someone else entirely. The naive, soft-hearted woman will be replaced with a fucking warrior. The new Dollface, the new me, will be more than a pretty doll.

My breath came in silent gasps as I pressed my palms into my bent knees. I felt the searing pain that had momentarily singed my senses . Everytime air hit the cuts it would send a pang of fire in the back of my shoulder. Remembering myself I straightened my posture, willing myself to remain undisturbed by the event. I couldn't let Felix see. Not yet. Not when he was not facing me with a flash of those newly haunted eyes, before it was masked yet again.

"You did wonderful, Dollface. I'm sorry we must go to such lengths." Felix whispered, his voice ever so slightly waning, his brow furrowed.

I forced a smile.

Felix's gaze lingered on me a little too long, at my fractured smile. His lingering gaze heated my skin and quickened my pulse, even with where we were. He is still Felix. I must be going mad.

"Thank you. ." My words came out sharper than I'd intended, but I couldn't let him look at me that way any longer. Despite all of this utter bullshit, I had empathy for Felix. He seems to be brainwashed by Father Gurevich's twisted ideals. He'd never understand, though. It just is much simpler to endure the worst in silence than to let anyone see what I'm really thinking. Including him.

He studied me for a moment, the intensity of his stare making my stomach tighten. It made me take a slow, drag of a breath, trying to steady myself.

*Do NOT feel sorry for him, Nat. He did this to you.*

Felix reached out, his fingertips brushing against my cheek . His hesitant touch felt like a safety net. "You don't have to be strong all the time, but I'm glad you are. That's how I know you're perfect for me."

My heart twisted, but I bowed my head, wishing away the tears threatening to fall. "I don't need to be stronger." I replied, keeping my eyes downcast on the floor. "I just need to be free."

So rather than withering, and bending-this moment will be a tool for my future self. A future self that will reign. One that confronts my own weaknesses, and challenges my own decisions.

# CHAPTER 14

*Felix*

L ast night wasn't the first night I'd spent in Natalya's cage, the steady rise and fall of her chest bringing me comfort. My giant arms are wrapped around her body, hoping I am giving her a sense of comfort. Lightbulbs flickered on the ceiling, giving the room a faint glow. The warmth of my Dollface against me attempts to ground my thoughts, but nothing can right now. Although, she is the only thing to come close to silencing my mind.

I promised myself, when I'd first known what I was going to do to her, that I wouldn't allow myself to second guess it. . She was a complication. A masterfully ethereal complication, one that could shred my world to pieces with a single tear. But then I smiled, knowing I got to have her as mine.

The moment she talked with me for the first time, her eyes friendly and bright, I knew for certain it was only a matter of time before she wrapped herself around me like a boa. I'm not immune, I am but a man. A sinner. And now here I am—caught in a web of addiction and feral need, where love and torment bled into one another. I took a sharp inhale, trying to calm my pulse.

The cleansing was the only way. The thought was like my blade. Sharp, and painful. I had known from the start that I would have to hurt her. Not because I wanted to, but because it was the only avenue to our eternal salvation together. She will understand. She would hate me, then love me again. That was part of the price to pay. Part of the price I had to pay to keep Father Gurevich in his own lane when it came to my Dollface. Natalya was mine. Mine to punish. Mine to cleanse. Mine to hold.

Tonight is the last night of phase two of the cleansing. It'd already nearly been a week. My remarkably tough little doll has held her head high for the whole week. With each slice of her skin, I can see the anger and pain in her eyes-but my Nat is too perfect to let that show. The cleansing must be working. More than it had for Tati, even. Tati seems broken into submission, but not my Nat. No, Natalya seems to be strengthening into submission. That doesn't mean I don't hate hurting her, no matter the purpose. But, Father Gurevich knows best. He knows the true desires of our Lord and what we must do.

Holding her every night has been incredible, and I suspect it adds to her strength. Further proving she will willfully belong to me . There are things I do still miss about my Dollface that I haven't been blessed with in a while, though. Her laugh, the very noise that made me ache with a longing I can't begin to explain. Her hands, with her short little painted nails. The ones that caressed the outlines of my heart with her touch. She was everything I'd always longed for. And in a fantastic gift of life, she had fallen for me too. At least, it seemed so more each day. . She had traveled and immersed herself in my world, unknowingly binding herself to me. A person incapable of loving her without hurting her. But I had no choice.

She hated me for a while, yes. But yet she would be safe here. Safe from the kind of danger Father Gurevich possesed deep in his old bones, the kind that clung to the father like a bad omen. My

Dollface wouldn't know what to do, or what I had to become in order to protect her, but it was the only way. It had always been the only way.

A single tear slid down my cheek. I wiped it away angrily. How dare I.

What if Natalya never truly forgives me? What if she never chooses to stay on her free will? She shouldn't. And yet... I cannot stop the ache that punched me in my chest, the weight of what I was about to do for phase three of the cleansing.

I placed a light kiss on Natalya's head, and knew I needed to get up and speak with Gurevich about my Dollface's graduation to phase three. I'd despised marring her glorious flesh. Alas, a sick piece of me also felt a hunger and possessiveness of me marking my doll. It made her mine even more.

I slowly slipped away from Nat and the mattress, heading for the door. My heart hammered in my chest. I am a man on a mission, swaying between the woman I loved and the only father I had ever known. The further away from the basement I got, the more it hurt. The more I regretted it and had to smother it down. The closer I got to where Father Gurevich was, the more it felt like I was suffocating. But I couldn't afford to fail on my part, not yet. Not until it was over.

-

◆ ◆ ◆

Father Gurevich stood in the poorly lit cathedral, the scent of candles and wine heavy in the air, a scent that seemed to taint everything it touched. His eyes were fixed on the wooden crucifix hanging above the altar, then he'd glance down at his bottle of wine. I'd suspected Gurevich used to struggle with alcoholism, but for a Priest that'd be insanely inappropriate.
His eyes kept glancing at that cross, the battered figure of our Lord

crucified. He muttered to himself, almost as if the words were coming from somewhere deep within, and as if no one was meant to hear.

"Sin." he muttered, his frail fingers brushing over the wine bottle, "Sin is a price. A price paid in bloodletting. In torture and suffering."

The upper layer of the Cathedral was empty, apart from the singular Priest now kneeling at his altar. Father Gurevich looked lost and the stench of the wine grew stronger the closer I had gotten. Natalya was pure. She didn't need this- but she is exactly the kind of soul Father Gurevich craved.

With slowed, deliberate steps, I approached him. His face was flushed, stoney as though the voice of reason had long since left him. His eyes, though, were cold. Filled to the brim with malice. He has a madness that few could understand.

"Felix," he said, his voice almost a slur. "You seek to covet her. But coveting is a sin. You want her forgiveness, it is required by us or our creator. Although, people don't offer it much. It's a trick of the gullible, a way to avoid the truths of life. The truth is that sin must be purged, and forgiveness is the one requirement we may never give. We must suffer until we agree to bend."

I knelt beside him, reaching out and taking the win. He moved his hand toward me, his fingers stabling himself on my shoulder, cold and brittle.

"I know you've sinned, Felix," he continued, his words filled with a mixture of anger and grief.. "I can smell it on you. Like the stench of death. You think you can come here, into my Cathedral, and I won't know? No." He leaned closer, clumsily. His breath wafted toward me with the scent of booze. "You cannot escape your desires for your little Dollface, Felix. Not any of them. So, if you wish to keep her and go unpunished, you'd better do this right."

"You Felix, you think," Father Gurevich grumbled, "that faith is a cure. A numbing that soothes the pain in the soul. But it is not, my boy. It is the flames of hell. Our cleansings are agony, and they must be." He stood, his arm wrapped around my body, using me as leverage. It'd been years since I'd seen him this way. Since Tati's cleansing. "Do you see the price of eternal life, Felix? Do you realize what must be done?"

"You want her salvation?" Father Gurevich straightened, his eyes gleaming. "Then you will learn that salvation is an expensive request."

Father Gurevich stood more firmly now, and retrieved an iron of sorts from the floor near the altar, the metal of it catching in the light like the gleam of hell's finest jewelry. My eyes widened, my heart pounded in my chest. The old bastard is going to brand her, like he did Tati.

"No, Father, please. You'd promised me I was in charge of her cleansing." I begged, but my words fell on deaf ears for the Priest.

Father Gurevich drew himself closer to my ear, his face twisted in a sadistic expression of pleasure. "Oh, but you are Felix. Who do you think will be branding the girl? Surely not me. No one can cheat around the wrath of the cleansing. You're aiming to rob your Natalya of the purity required to be a part of this family. How selfish of you, *Doc*. Tati couldn't escape it, I had to do it to my Darling Dolly. Now you must inflict this on yours. It is for their own good, remember that. But through this offering of their sinners flesh and blood, they will understand the magnitude of their offenses."

With a shaky hand, he places the branding iron in my other hand. The feel of it shot well forgotten memories to the forefront of my mind. The last time this touched any part of my flash, it was for my own branding. Anxiety made my stomach wretched at what he was asking of me. Especially to my perfect Dollface.

Father Gurevich took in my expression, letting out a fiendish chuckle. He is wholly unfazed. Father Gurevich grinned, his voice lethal, almost born from malice. "Their cleansings are vital, Felix. It is not enough to confess. You must suffer in the name of your salvation. Only then will your soul be pure."

I don't know how I'd never seen it before.   Each of his declarations were a confession of his distorted vision of God's will. Father Gurevich was beyond holiness himself, and he knew it. He was merely a tool—a tool of torture, of cruelty and damnation. And me? Well, I was only now beginning to question him. I never had before, but he had been all I had ever known. The only family I'd had since I was a small boy. Me being a broken, small boy is what made It easy to believe him.  Now as I think of searing my sweet Natalya's flesh with this branding iron, seeds of doubt plant themselves into my thoughts.

We should make our way down to the basement, Father. Our dolls should be awake," I whispered. "Let's get this over with, for Natayla's  soul is one step closer to belonging here with us."

But I now  felt it was all a lie. Which made me sick to my core, but I knew better than to refuse. This cathedral was not a place I'd want to be for eternity. It is a place of torment and regardless of these thoughts flooding me, we walk down to the basement.

# CHAPTER 15

*Dollface*

**M**y eyes blink open, the steel bars of the cage slowly come into vision. My body aches, like I've been sleeping on the world's shittiest mattress for days. Oh wait, I have. For weeks, actually. A metallic smell permeates the air, mixing with the lingering taste of dread on my tongue. My mind isn't so focused at first, but reality slams into me quickly—It's been fourteen days. I'm still a captive. The noises around me are suffocating, but it's the warning of what's to come, I know it. Today is the last day of phase two of my cleansing. Dread suffocates my chest, making it more difficult to breathe. What will be my final day of phase two's so-called reward.Each time I wake up in this cage, it cuts me deeper, the reminder that Felix has betrayed me, and I'm nothing but a possession.

Felix has been holding me nightly still. He's been doing his best to comfort me after my body aches and burns in sheer irritations all over the skin of my back. First the lashings of week one, then the carvings for bloodletting of this week. What could be next? I appreciate his sentiment, truly, but he is also the one who inflicts such agony on me. From my understanding, it is so Gurevich isn't the one. Felix keeps reiterating that to me, the fact he is attempting to lessen my blows. The strangest thing is that

I actually believe him. I'm either a total idiot, or the Stockholm Syndrome has fully set in now.

It must have, because every night in his arms almost erases the events of the day. I've come close to burying my face in his chest and fully allowing myself to let go. If I have nothing else here, I could allow myself one thing. One lifeline to keep me grounded. That doesn't squash the fear for what is to come, though. Even if Felix tries to make it easier for me.

That's when I hear footsteps, and glance over at the door to see Felix and Father Gurevich entering the basement. Felix has something in his hand. It's long, and metal with an oddly flat end. The end isn't just flat, it appears as though it's shaped into... letters, maybe? Then that's when Felix sticks that end of the rod into the fireplace, I'm assuming to-"Heat up." I mumble to myself.

Why would he need to-*Oh, no.* Well, now I know what today's agenda is. I think I'm going to be branded like fucking cattle. My back is an absolute atrocity right now, so I can't imagine where they'll decide to put it. I know Tati has done this before, but even when we were both disrobed her hair was down, and we wore undergarments. Which means, the branding will be anywhere not immediately seen.

I don't allow my initial panic to set in. Felix will be instructed to punish me, and the look in his eyes is always heartbreaking. Much how they appear now as he unlocks my cage and can barely meet my gaze.

"Hello, Felix." I greet him with a soft smile. "Branding, huh?" My words make him sigh and press a quick, soft kiss against my forehead.

"I'm sorry, Dollface." He admits, his stare finally locking in mine. The ice of his eyes is as hauntingly gorgeous as they have always been. Am I crazy, or do I want to kiss him? Damn captivity brain-I've seen too much true crime for this, so I shake it away.

He walks me near the fireplace instead today, instructing me to kneel there instead, likely due to the methods of graduating from phase two. "I have something to help you, Dollface." Felix mutters, as he brings a wine bottle to my lips and orders, "Drink, Natalya."

"You both consume large amounts of alcohol for being so religious." The snark in my tone was unintentional, but I'd be justified nonetheless. "What's the occasion this time?" I question him, after gulping down what must have been equivalent to two glasses of wine.

Felix's expression twists into mild annoyance as he claims, "It's for the pain, Dollface. Now, no more questions. You want this over with, don't you?" His masculine and spicy, woody scent invades my senses every time he gets closer. Since when did I notice his scent? We have got to halt  the aftercare, for religious torture-cuddles. The affection is messing with my head. Skewing my perception immensely. It feels like I've been hexed. Maybe this bullshit does rewire your brain, but it had to be the trauma. It's definitely not a healthy bond we have formed.

My  heart began racing as I knelt, the fire from the fireplace flickered all around us  like fireflies in the night. Felix stood near, removing the hot iron from the fire. He was speaking, his lips were moving- but I couldn't hear him. I could barely hear Felix over the pounding of my own heart  in my ears.

Behind me, Felix  lifted the hot iron. The iron glowed with how hot it had become, shimmering like gold.  The design read, Dollface. It was intended  to sear more than just my skin; it would burn the mark of this cult. It would also burn Felix's nickname for me, I'd be branded as forever his. Did he design this, or was it Gurevich?

My  eyes flickered to where the iron stuck out of his hand, searching desperately for Felix. My friend, the man I'd grown feelings and a dependency for. This isn't how it was supposed to be. No, not this. But here he was, about to brand me. Ruin me.

"Natalya," his voice was soft, but tinged with a note of something else. "You've now completed phase two of the cleansing. And now, you will be branded, in an act to show where you belong, and how far you've come. Do you understand?"

My throat constricted. I swallowed hard, but only gave him silence. There was nothing I could say. Yes I understand what you are doing, but not the purpose-other than severe illness. Other than being brainwashed by a cult-minded Priest.

Felix stepped closer, his movements deliberate, like the slice of a sword cutting through the silence. His voice rang out with intention and strength. Strength I'd needed.

"3..2..1." His eyes bore into the back of my skull, I could feel it. "No, this isn't right. I can't do this.." The iron clatters to the ground. "You're mine Dollface, and I don't want to hurt you anymore. I was wrong. So wrong." I inhale a deep gasp, it's everything I'd wanted from him. Shock fills me, but it's short lived as the realization sets in that Gurevich will be the one to brand me.

Father Gurevich growled, and glared at Felix. "You dare defy the requirements of the cleansing, Felix?" he spit in his iciest tone.

Felix wasn't listening to Father Gurevich. He dropped to his haunches in front of me, his gaze never wavering from mine. "Natalya, look at me," he demanded. "Please. I don't want to hurt you for him anymore. How did I ever buy into this? It took hurting you to make me question myself..Listen, Dollface, I know I've done a lot already. But even a mentally unhinged psycho like me has limits."

Tears fell down my face as I reached out to trace his cheek with my thumb. I wanted to believe him. To trust him. I had wanted to believe we could escape this place together. To leave behind all of the darkness and pain and the fear that had controlled Felix for so many years. But I was smart enough to know what would happen if he didn't do as he was asked. Father Gurevich would punish them both, then they might die there. Right in the Cathedral basement.

I think I love you, Felix," I whispered, my voice cracking. "I love you, but—" I swallowed— "you doing this is the only way you can ensure we make it out of here in one piece". I don't think I was lying, either. In a way, I do love Felix-as sick as it may be. He just proved he loved me, too.

No." Felix shook his head, his eyes glossy with unshed emotion. "I can't-"

Father Gurevich, stepped forward with unfiltered rage, raised the iron in his hands.. The heat was unbearable, and the scent of burning flesh was around us, as my screams broke through the air, grounding both Felix and I into reality once again.

"Stop," Felix growled, gripping the iron, his eyes filled with fury. Maybe even a bit of concern.

My breath caught deep in my throat. What is Felix doing? He's going to get himself hurt, or killed.

In what seemed like a nanosecond, Father Gurevich raised his hand gripping the iron, and smacked Felix to the ground with it. "You have forgotten your place, boy. And now, you must lay in the bed you made! I will be in charge of your sweet Natalya's cleansing!" He commanded, as Felix slowly stood to his feet, cupping a hand to his cheek. Did the iron graze him there?

"Felix.." I'd cried, noting the uneven burn on his cheekbone. I wanted to scream, to break things, to kill Father Gurevich. But all I could do in this moment was watch as Father Gurevich commanded Felix into a chair, and threatened to give him a lashing all night if he didn't behave himself. Fellix's eyes were locked with mine almost the entire time, his expression one of regret. It only made Father Gurevich angrier. I can remain stoic, and strong for my own punishments-but not for Felix's. Nor could he for mine anymore, but we'd have to- for now.

Once he was finished reprimanding Felix, Father Gurevich turned back to face me, a snake-like grin curling his thin lips. "Now, for Felix's little doll. You've finally earned another punishment. Well, technically it was Felix but I have to show my boy how serious I am about my word. Something he should know already."

Felix swallowed, and turned sickly pale. My breaths came in frantic gasps. I could feel the heat of the iron closing in on me, the room around blurring, until I saw nothing but Felix's face.

But before the iron touched my skin again, a hand gripped the rod.. Felix, broken and defiant, said "I'll do it, Father. Move away. This is my girl."

Father Gurevich smiled, a shit eating grin tarnishing his face. "I knew you'd come around." He says to Felix.

I took it all in, my heart thumping in my chest, as Felix feigned losing his fight. I understand why he has to. For a moment, I'd wondered if mercy killing might be in our futures. Felix's eyes met mine again, and I knew we'd have each other.

The insanity around us nearly disappeared. Nothing mattered except for us in this moment, and I saw the promise in Felix's eye. Regardless of what he wanted, Felix knew what he had to do. He pressed the hot iron to the back of my neck, and was instructed to hold it there for ten, long seconds.

Felix's hands were shaking as he crouched down and scooped me up, his breaths uneven. The room was silent, Father Gurevich left after Felix branded me. My breaths were shallow, and I winced at the random moments of contact when my hair grazed the brand on the back of my neck , my body depleted and sore. .

"I'm sorry," Felix murmured, his jaw clenched, he was angry. . His mouth pressed to the top of my head as he carried me into my cage, and placed me on my mattress. "I never wanted this," he admitted. "Tomorrow begins phase three. The final phase."

My eyes were raw from the tears, mine landed on Felix's, but we didn't speak right away. Instead, he clenched his jaw, and grit his teeth. As if he were trying to control the tornado of emotions threatening to consume him. The silence between us stretched for uncomfortably long, as we laid down and took me into his embrace. My face was buried into the fabric of his tee shirt, on his hard chest.

"You didn't have a choice," I reminded him, my voice steady. "I'd rather it be you, as fucked as it is." My hands gripped onto him tightly, and I pressed a kiss to his cheek. It'd been the first kiss I'd initiated between us.

Felix heaved in a breath. The past few weeks were likely playing through his mind— the moment he'd been forced to brand me. The sounds of his body hitting the floor, after standing up to Gurevich, was on my mind. The very second Father Gurevich attempted to take matters into his own hands, Felix remembered why he told me it had to be himself to inflict the punishments. I'd thought he'd signed our death warrants today with his outburst, but at the same time, it felt great that he stood up for me. It showed me that my Felix does exist.

"How have I been so brainwashed? Look at all I've done. I've given you lashings, carved your beautiful skin-my whole life is a lie, Dollface. Was everything else really okay with me, or was I convincing myself?," he asked, running a hand over his face, his frustration evident. His eyes held so much guilt, and they fell to my neck, brushing my hair away from the brand.

I winced from the pain slightly, anticipating his touch, but when I looked up at him again, there was a spark of something else

I'd let show in my eyes. I am not angry with him, not my Felix. He didn't need to apologize — not like this. I needed him to be strong, and to let me forget for a while tonight.

"That part is over now, Felix," I reminded him, my voice soft. "We're both alive. That's all that matters right now, and I know how you can help me."

He freezes, and swallows-his face turning down to look at mine. I'm still wrapped tightly in his arms, glancing back up at him. A soft smile finds its way onto my lips. "How?" He questions hesitantly.

My hand reached up to comb my fingers through his very short hair, it was buzzed when I'd arrived. He's let the top grow a little these past few weeks. "Make me feel like we are the only people in this world right now. That nothing else is real. Make me forget, Felix."

My pulse grew unsteady, and my heart thudded in my chest. Only this time, it wasn't from fear. Warmth filled me, as anticipation fled through my body. Felix leaned in closely, close enough that I could almost taste his cinnamon breath. His lips grazed mine lightly, brushing against my own for the first time ever. Heat filled my core, as both of our breathing became ragged, and then his lips met mine.

# CHAPTER 16

*Felix*

A m I dreaming, or is my Dollface letting me kiss her? Her pouty lips are softer than I could have ever imagined. It began with an almost slow, hesitant exchange of kisses. I just hadn't been sure she knew what she sas asking, but once our lips fully touched I was gone.

At first our mouths were exploring each other's, followed by her soft sighs and groans. It caused a need and possessiveness to spread through my body. My hands began gently cupping the back of her slender neck, to pull her in deeper, and traced the sensual curves of her body. Fuck, I wanted more. I wanted to consume her, devour her. It created a desire to keep my word to aid in her protection and success with this cleansing, but it also fed the monster. The word *mine* kept echoing in my head. That's when I realized I would protect her, from everyone but me.

Natalya broke our kiss, panting, her lips swollen from the contact with mine. What a delicious sight it was. "Is that what you were looking for, Dollface?" I asked, releasing the breath I hadn't realized I was holding. My eyes searched hers, looking for any signs of regret.

"Perfect." She exhaled, her face flushing. Which causes me to smile down at her-as I do slow, tender strokes down her back.

"Good, we should do it again sometime." I offer her with my best wink.

Natalya chuckles, and the sound causes my heart to swell. I want to hear more of that precious sound. It isn't something I've heard much of lately. It is a shame that I know tomorrow will be a day of pure hell. It is the start of Phase three, after all.

"Felix," My beautiful doll whispers, laying her pretty little head onto my chest again.

"Yes, baby?" I wonder, gently toying with her hair, her strawberry scent driving me crazy.

"Thank you, for this. For what it's worth- I'd always liked you. You are the only reason this is more tolerable." She admits. Her words should make me feel warm and fuzzy, but they slice through me. Look at what I've done. I did not lie when I said I'd try to help her; I will not let Gurevich harm her. But I won't let her go, either. She can escape him, and all of this cleansing bullshit- but never me. Natalya Lane is mine. She can go back home temporarily, but I will never be too far behind.

◆ ◆ ◆

After waking from what must have been the best sleep one could have on the mattress of a Cathedral's basement, I looked down at the woman in my arms. The feel of the exhale of her breaths against me warms me, until I glance up to meet the stern gaze of Father Gurevich. My lips twitch in annoyance at seeing the old loon. He doesn't say anything, instead he clicks his tongue against his teeth, and strides away to set things up.

I wake up Natalya by placing tender kisses to her head and cheeks. Today is going to be difficult for her, for both of us. The first day of phase three is here , and I can't imagine her wanting anything to do with me after this.

Her pretty grey eyes blink up at me, a sleepy smile playing on her lips. One that fades when I remind her of what's to come. "Let's go, Dollface." I whisper as I walk her, hand in hand, to Father Gurevich.

"Kneel for me, Doll." I instruct gently, my thumb reassuringly stroking the softness of her cheek. "Welcome to day one of phase three." My expression tries to convey that I don't wish this upon her, but we both know why it must go on.

Her eyes reassure me before they lower, and I mutter "Good girl." Stepping back to really take her in, and command her. To relay the next steps. It is true, I still don't wish for her physical harm, but we must proceed.

There is also a deeply buried part of me that still eats up her submission. Likely the years of brainwashing by Gurevich since I was a boy, but regardless, It feels right from her. Especially from her. It has the two sides of me shredding apart my brain. They're going to war inside of me.

"Get on with it, Felix." Orders Father Gurevich, while he pours thick, red liquid into glasses. "You are beginning to try my patience." Tati is out of her cage today, but is not participating, only cleaning our blades of the remnants of last week's blood.

I address Natalya, really taking in her pristine form. Even with all of her new scars, she is exquisite. "Welcome to phase three of your cleansing, Dollface. Congratulations, you have made it to your final week."

*The cleansing; Phase Three:*

1. *Kneel and say a prayer, thanking Father Gurevich and Felix. Daily.*

2. *You will confess your daily sinful thoughts, while being flogged.*
3. *Consume "corpse medicine"-aka Blood. Daily.*

*The Romans once believed you could cure ailments by drinking the blood of fallen gladiators, and physicians believed blood elixirs could cure ailments. Including rid you of the last of your sins.*

4. *You will practice Babylonian skull cures for the week, in which you will sleep by a human skull for the week. It is believed that if there are any spirits to exercise-it will. You will kiss the skull 7 times before bed.*

*Rules and Punishments:*

1. *If you do not sound gracious, you will begin again-until we see fit.*
2. *If you have nothing to confess, we will assume you're a liar, and burn the tip of your tongue.*
3. *If you refuse the corpse medicine you will graduate from blood to eating the cremation dust from the deceased.*
4. *If you fail this, we will tie you to a tree in the forest, for each day. With this Siberian weather, you will get frostbite.*

*Graduation night:*

*Graduation night you will be mock crucified, for all to see. Each of us in the room will drive one nail through your palm or foot. You will remain there until morning. Congratulations, and welcome to our family.*

Natalya sucked in a harsh breath after hearing what is expected of phase three. Her pretty eyes grew wild, and she swallowed, never leaving her position. *Strong girl*, I think to myself. It only made me admire her more. Everything about my Dollface was perfect, but this week would prove difficult.

Though, her breath  still had seemed too shallow as I had announced the new rules for the week. The air felt thick, and I'd noticed Tati eyeing us with a horror stricken expression.

My heart thumped, all of our eyes were on her, awaiting a reaction- but she barely noticed. Her fingers tightened around the sleeve of her sweater.  Her knuckles turned  white as she noted every word out of my mouth.

" The punishments are more severe this week," Father Gurevich piped in, breaking the silence. His cold, assessing gaze sweeping over Natalya.  "Any disobedience will be punished." He'd said. The heartless fucker.

Natalya's chest rose and fell, goosebumps appeared to have pebbled my doll's skin.  I could tell the weight of phase three was suffocating her. Her pouty lips parted, but no sound emerged —just a sharp intake of breath. Schooling herself, my Dollface composed herself like a pro, and squared her shoulders.

"Corpse Medicine?" she'd pondered under her breath, only so I could hear. She likely wonders whose blood it will be. It nearly doesn't matter; though, consuming blood is consuming blood.

Her eyes darted upward, desperately locking with mine,some form of reassurance from the others, maybe as some form of reassurance. Then, she'd lowered her head, her hair tumbling over her shoulders-and she began her prayer. I'm aware of how sick and wrong it is, but it being addressed to me, made my heart sing. She could never know the small pleasures I'd take.

Her prayer was beautiful, I'm sure it helped her along knowing it'd be for me. At least, that's what I'll allow myself to believe.

I stood before her, my gaze observing her lovingly, but intensely. Father Gurevich stood to my right, mostly focusing on Tati. He had just wanted to oversee it all. His presence stalked the space of the basement  like a shadow-one that'd never leave me alone.

My heart pounded, each beat more prominent than the last, thudding against my ribcage. I was nervous, this week has big stakes. The flickering lights from the candles around the room cast long shadows across the stone walls. All that seemed to matter in this moment was her, Natalya. My Dollface.

"Do not make the mistake of believing phase three will be as easily digested as the others," I'd said calmly, but I could still only imagine the chill it'd shot up her spine. "The new rules have been set, but thus far you're doing a fantastic job. Now, begin your confession. You've prayed enough. " I reminded her.

"Now, my sweet doll, what do you have to confess to us?" I probe, although, I believe I know. I'm sure her thoughts recently have been similar to mine.

"I-I'm not sure, Felix. I've not been anywhere, not had much to do around here." Natalya answers, her gaze never lifting from the floor.

"Oh, I think you have something. Remember the rules, Dollface." I reprimanded, crossing my arms. Her gaze sprung up to meet mine, while a smirk played at my lips. " Tick..Tock..Natalya, darling."

"Forgive me Felix, and Father Gurevich-For I have sinned.." Natalya doesn't break eye contact with me as she rambles in about her forsaking God this week, and her lustful thoughts during our kiss. Ones I'd had as well, but our time will come soon enough. The thought draws a devilish grin to my lips, but I quickly wipe it away in an attempt for Father Gurevich to not see.

"Very good, Natalya." I praise, then turn and lift a glass of thick, red liquid for her corpse medicine. At least she shares a blood type with what used to be Hana. While we don't have access to the blood of Christ, I was indeed a doctor. I had access to many blood bags in the hospital. I'd brought them to the Cathedral freezer for this very purpose many times for Father Gurevich. We'd eventually run out, I couldn't take too much. It would have been too noticeable. Now, we use the blood of those who were not strong or obedient enough to survive their cleansings. After their sins killed them, we'd drain them dry, and freeze their blood. It begins as unholy blood, but we bless it-like the water. I'd imagine this once belonged to the woman from nearly a year ago. I hadn't desired her, but Father Gurevich claimed she was possessed-that we were to help her. Her name was Hana. She'd come here from Japan with her long-time boyfriend, Val. Hana was a fighter, for a quiet woman. She had promise, but the loss of her precious Val held her back.

Father Gurevich had claimed her pre-marital relationship is what brought about her possession. We only seem to recruit women, he'd always claimed they were men's original temptation. That they'd all needed cleansing. Any man who gave himself to a woman before commitment under God, Father Gurevich has always been deemed them as weak. Unholy. Rotten, like old fruit. He'd likely say the same of my Dollface and I, if he knew just how intense my infatuation was.

"It's time you've had your corpse medicine, my darling Natalya." I say smoothly, gently guiding her chin up with the pad of my forefinger. The look of disgust flashed across her face, and then it was gone. Yes, this was disgusting, however, I'm quite desensitized. At least she wasn't the one in charge of draining and bagging blood from a limp corpse. She'd be dry heaving in the corner. The truth is, I'd been corrupted by Father Gurevich's twisted cult mind long before then. Draining Hana's blood was nothing to me, but draining my dear Natalya's would be. I refuse to allow that to become actuality.

"Felix-is that real blood? Whose blood is that?" Natalya stutters, swallowing wide eyed.

I brush her hair behind her shoulders, and remind her of the repercussions of not completing what is asked of her at this stage. "Now really isn't the time for questions, Doll. I love you, and that's why I must be callous about this. I will tell you all about it later." My lips brush against her ear, as I raise the glass to her lips. "Go on, drink."

After giving me what felt like the longest side-eye in the world, she looked back at the red liquid, and gulped it down. "Good job, Natalya. You've done great, now don't throw it up." I pat her shoulder and straighten. What does she do? She throws it up.

"I'm almost impressed," Admits Gurevich, his slow clap echoing throughout the room. "I'd thought surely she'd refuse, and we'd get to add some excitement to today. The only excitement I've gotten is vomit on my floor." He takes slow strides over to us, to study Natalya before saying, "You may just belong here after all. Felix knows what he's doing, but you have to keep drinking it until you can keep it in your stomach. Otherwise, it does you no good." Then, he takes a nearby seat to see Natalya's reaction to the second cup of blood.

She throws up again, and again. An infuriating amount of times. "You know what this means, don't you, doll?" I question, cupping her cheek. "You have to eat the cremation ash now."

"Now THIS is what I was hoping to see." Father Gurevich gleams, clasping his hands together. "My money is on her spitting it out. "

"You want me to eat what was once a person's bones?" Natayla queries with a strong aversion to the sheer idea of such a thing.

"Yes, dear, and if you do not-you know there are consequences. Do you wish to suffer?" Father Gurevich answered for me. He must be quite bored today.

"No, Father Gurevich." Natalya answers, a look in her eyes defiant. He must have noticed, because he gave a dry chuckle and retrieved the ern filled with the ashes of everything but Hana's skull. He dips out a spoon of them into a glass, then fills the glass with wine, and stirs it.

"To make it go down easier." He smirks, and hands her the glass. Her eyes glare daggers at him, as she tightens her delicate hand around it, and brings it to her lips.

"Mmm, ashy wine. Why thank you, Father. Can't imagine where you'd have come up with such a delicacy-"Her words are cut short when a crack sounds through the air. At first I'd thought my eyes had deceived me, but what I saw before me had been very real. My Natalya, sprawled across the floor, her hand clutching her ever reddening cheek. It'd be swollen and bruised by morning, and I see red.

I grip Father Gurevich by his collar, and slam his back into the table, never letting loose on my grip. Snarling, I demand, "Who do you think you are, putting your decrepit hands on MY woman?"

The fear in Father Gurevich's eyes is palpable. His breaths releasing on a wheeze, he must have hit the table hard. "Need I remind you who you're speaking to, boy?" He grits.

I scoff. "Need I remind your nearly crippled ass who is in charge of MY Natalya's cleansing, Father?" I really made sure to put some emphasis on that one for the old fuck. There must be a little crazy in me after all, because I'd enjoy nothing more than to break his brittle neck. There would be satisfaction like no other to feel him crumple at the hands of my palms, but I won't be him any longer. Won't be comparable, so I released him. Against my better judgment, for sure.

Father Gurevich's stare burns holes into the side of my head, "If you put your hands on me again, you will both be crucified at the end of the week, because you've clearly forgotten who's raised you. Now clean this mess up, and proceed."He spits. pulling his blade from under his cassock. I have no doubt in my mind he'd do away with us, without blinking. He'd gut us all like fish and feast on our entrails.

Natalya spends what feels like an eternity scrubbing herself and the floor, then we begin again. This time, with only mild gagging she consumes her Corpse Medicine. The knowledge that I can do nothing but watch makes me as useless as I feel. I don't deserve this beautiful woman. It helps to relieve some of the tension knowing we are inching closer to finishing this hell. Although, when Father Gurevich pulls out the skull and hands it to me, some of Hana's hair is still attached in strings. Which is terrifying.

Natalya momentarily quivers, but doesn't react as much as I'd expected her to. Her poker face can be phenomenal. Her lack of reaction seems to please Father Gurevich. He approaches her, pauses, and his eyes study her with cruel amusement. He seemed to enjoy her desperation, and her perceived submission to the cruelty.

"Good, good," he said, his voice lethal, but the threat beneath it couldn't be missed, "You are learning your place, girl. Your soul may be saved after all."

# CHAPTER 17

*Dollface*

In just a few minutes, I will be crucified. Today is the final day of these mind games. The final twenty-four hours of this personal hell. A cult run by a fucking Priest, either to satiate real thoughts stemming from mental illness-or his sadistic needs being met. I know that elderly sad sack of flesh enjoys it. I have seen the sick glints in his wrinkled eyes.

The final week of the cleansing was rough. I don't know how I survived it. Seven days of miraculously keeping down the consumption of blood. Seven days of praying to that sorry excuse of a Priest, Gurevich. A week of my life was spent on gut-wrenching hell, in an attempt to survive.

Then Felix and I can get the hell out of here. Out of this cage. Away from this Godless Cathedral, and far from Siberia. My Nana and Pappy are probably worried to death right now. They'll never allow me to leave their sights again.

Father Gurevich unlocks the cage today. Likely due to the fact Felix has taken it upon himself to have nightly aftercare, and sleepovers. It does help having him by my side. He is the only reason I feel remotely safe, but today I feel ill. My palms are about to be nailed to a fucking cross.

"Come on Dollface, last day." Felix whispers, placing a tattooed hand on my lower back in an attempt to usher me forward.

Directing my question at Father Gurevich, I ask "Where's the cross? I don't see it anywhere." He ignores me. Sometimes it seems like I don't exist to him, and other times he is far too invested. Only, he's often solely invested in moments when he sees a harsh punishment in my near future. I'm sure he will be fully fixated and present while nailing my palm or ankle.

I flick my gaze to Felix. How can he be so handsome, even now? It's unfair really. "Felix?" I ask, hoping he gives me something.

" It's upstairs, Dollface. The crucifixion is sacred, and Father Gurevich has always believed God would want witnesses to his testimony. Your cleansing being witnessed is believed to be a thing of beauty. " Felix answers, his tone devoid of any shred of the amusement I had expected to see. His poker face is almost as good as mine, unless-parts of him still believe bits and pieces. He was brainwashed for years.

"Who's going to be watching?" I implore, genuinely curious. I had been under the impression that all of the other women had died.

"My brothers," answers Felix, "Father Gurevich raised us together. They were cleansed as well.

"How many brothers do you have?" I don't know what's more shocking, that Felix has brothers he hasn't really mentioned-or that they're a part of this fucked up cult too.

"Three. We aren't brothers by blood, but Gurevich took us all under his wing as boys. There were four of us, but one of us-well, he's gone. " Felix's voice cracked, talking about how his brothers really got to him. It may be the first time I've seen him this way over anyone who wasn't me.

"That's right. His sin got the better of him. The weak, piss poor excuse of a lamb of God." Remarked Father Gurevich. His words sent mg blood boiling. I'd had to bite the inside of my cheek to avoid saying something that might get me killed.

"I'm sorry, Felix." I say softly , as I place a gentle hand on his arm.

"It's okay Dollface. We uh-we should head upstairs. They're waiting for us." He says as he laces our fingers and we pace up the staircase once more.

-

Upon reaching the room for attending mass in the Cathedral, I spotted them. Three men sitting in the front pew, facing the cross. Felix did mention Father Gurevich took them all in, but what he didn't touch on much was how they'd all quite obviously had different mothers. All three appeared to be half Russian, or Eastern European-but that is where their physical similarities end.  It's kind of unfair, because they're all fairly good looking. This is going to be so strange-having them watch me be crucified. The strangest part is that they all seem like this is normal to them, none of them have any reaction to anything around us. Including the giant wooden cross. Maybe they all just have really good poker faces.

 "Dollface, these are my brothers-Kai, Nikolai, and Malik." Felix smiles the first real smile I'd seen from him in days, as he ushers me over to them. "Guys, this is my Natalya."

"I see why you call her Dollface," Kai says with a hint of a smirk. "Lovely to meet you, *Natalya*." He addresses me.

"It's nice to meet all of you too-even if it is here."I try my best to form a tight lipped smile. Now wouldn't be the best time to go shitting on their Priest Daddy's cult.

Turning my head, I gaze up at the cross.  It stands a tall seven feet before the pews, perfect for holding up a person. Dark red-brown stains and etches from who knows what tarnish the wood. Such a classic symbolism of what I'm assuming is a significant story in their faith, yet it is being used for evil today. None of these men seem to realize it enough, though. They believe they're doing me some big favor, indoctrination me into their sick little cult.

Felix clears his throat. "It's time," he informs me, "We're going to reenact the crucifixion of Christ, as it is the proper symbolism. It's the only way we can ensure the completion of the cleansing, as believed by Father Gurevich." We make eye contact, I see the regret in then, but I know he doesn't have the best chances of stopping this. Not with all of these people.

Swallowing, I give him one last look and ask, "What is required of me?" He glances away, clenching his jaw. "What's wrong?"

"The Romans made our Lord disrobe to amplify humiliation-you must do the same. In front of everyone. You can keep your undergarments. You will then be held, by me- onto the cross. Then, a nail will be driven into each palm, and each ankle. Nailing you to the cross." He doesn't meet my watery gaze this time and whispers, "I'm sorry, Dollface. I really am. I do love you, this is the last day-remember that." Then he steps back, giving me the room I momentarily am allowed to be utterly mortified. I don't know his brothers, it was bad enough being a part of the corrupted game we have been playing.

"Get on with it, girl-No need to prolong it." Father Gurevich snips, patience has not yet seemed to be his strong suit. His leering eyes staring daggers right through me.

A sigh escapes my lips, as I downcast my eyes to the beautiful floors. *It's such a shame that a place like this is nothing but fallacy*, I think, as I begin to slip off my clothing. But before I can, I hear someone screech out a "No!" The voice is feminine. *Tati.*

My head snaps up, my eyes widening at the scene before me.

Tati has Father Gurevich pushed up against a pew, his knife in her hand-and the point of it is aimed at his chest. Right above his heart. My breath catches in my throat, and chaos erupts.

The sons, excluding Felix, stand abruptly. Only- Father Gurevich calls them off; like they're trained dogs. These grown ass men listen, too. They listen, and just act like carbon copy sheep puppets. It's almost mesmerizing, in a seriously disturbed way.

"Darling," Father Gurevich addresses her, "just what in God's name do you think you are doing?" The weird thing is, there doesn't seem to be any of the rage I'd expected from him. The rage he would most surely show me or Felix. He appears-hurt. Severely hurt by this. Interesting. I had always wondered about the nature of their relationship. There had to be a reason he chose to *cleanse* Tati.

"What I should have done a long time ago.. I cannot allow you to shove nails into a woman's palms. To crucify her. It was hard enough to watch the other things. But this cannot happen. Not again. I'm sorry, my *caxapok*." Tears well Tati's eyes as the hand with the dagger shakes.

"You won't kill me, darling. You love to hate me too much." Smirks Father Gurevich, closing his hand around Tati's, " Somebody needs more lashings. You've forgotten your place here."

My blood runs cold. Instead of handing him the blade, she grips it tightly and shoves it straight into his chest. Father Gurevich gasps in heaps of air. The loud crunch of it going straight through his chest cavity, and the gurgling noises from his mouth elicits nausea in the pit of my stomach, and I think I'm going to be sick. Felix's three brothers rush to Tati and Father Gurevich. The one they call Kai carries Tati away over his shoulder , while the other two crouch around Father Gurevich. They're saying something, but I can't make any of it out due to the sheer adrenaline and panic flooding my veins.

There isn't much time for me to process it all, though, because I'm being pulled by a frantic Felix toward the exit of the Cathedral. "Hurry, Dollface. We don't have much time." Felix shouted, gripping my hand tighter, as we burst outside through the doors. It's been so long since I've been outside, that even the frigid Siberian winter appeals to me.

"Felix, you did it! We're free, I'm free." I scream. It feels as though a million tons have been listed off of my chest. "Holy fuck. We're free, Felix," I exclaim, as we slide into his car and drive away.

"Yeah, Dollface, you are." He gives me a small smile. "You have a flight back to the United States in the morning."

My movements halt, and I'm confused with my own thoughts right now. I thought I'd be happy to hear that. I mean, I am happy, I'm fucking ecstatic to be out of that damn basement. Except-

"Will you come with me?" I almost hesitate to ask, but I'm not ready to leave Felix here. Not after everything, he went through all of this bullshit since he was a boy. He might thrive somewhere far the hell away from here.

"You'd want that? After-" He swallows, agony flashes across his face, before he quickly masks it away and clears his throat, "I thought you'd want to be far away from me too, Natalya. If I were you, that's what I'd want. I think you should go home to your grandparents alone. For your sake."

I don't know why his words disappoint me so much. Is it Stockholm Syndrome? Possibly. Is he the whole reason I ended up in that hell? Undoubtedly. Doesn't him saving me count for something, though? It should. Hell, maybe I've lost it. Maybe their cult ruined me after all. The only thing I'm sure of is that I can't leave him here.

Felix has never known normalcy, if he stays here it could be really bad for him. He could easily fall down the rabbit hole of everything he's done before, especially if I'm the only reason he'd ever seen it as wrong. That, and I kind of got used to his presence. Oh yeah, I will definitely need therapy after this.

"Yes. I want you to come with me, Felix. Please." I breathe out, stealing a glance at his side profile, and interlacing our fingers. He glances down at our fingers with a mix of confusion, and longing.

The car stops moving, we've reached his cabin. The same cabin I hadn't seen in three long weeks. It feels like three years. Felix is silent, as he opens my door for me and gently takes hold of my hand to help me out." Thank you," I say, as we near the front door.

❖ ❖ ❖

"So- why don't you want to come with me?" I ask him, "It could be really good for you."

"It's not that I don't want to come with you, Natalya. It is that I cannot." He admits, as he rinses his empty bowl, and sets it in the sink.  After we'd made it to the cabin, I'd called my Nana to say I'd be flying home tomorrow. I told her I'd tell her the details when I arrive home, after I'd gotten a scolding for scaring her half to death with the lack of communication and all. It was well deserved. I don't know what prevented me from telling her about Felix, but I didn't. Maybe I don't want to worry her more, or maybe it's something else. The same something else that grew while in the midst of turmoil. The same thing that made me invite him to come with me. He's human, too. What he did was fucked up and wrong, but he was brained washed for most of his life. Felix is a broken man, who was once a broken boy. Maybe I'm too empathetic toward him, or maybe I'm now broken too.

I pace over to his back, handing him my bowl and spoon as I inquire,"Why, can't you?"

Felix turns to face me, with a tick in his strong jaw. "Because you have to go alone, Natalya. You have to go alone."

My chest cracks, splitting a little. Why does he want to stay here? Is it because it's all he knows, or is it something else?

"No, Felix, you can come with me. I won't leave you in your own personal hell. I refuse. Please." I plead, but I fear it is falling upon deaf ears at this point. "At least tell me why." I'd shed tears, but I've shed them all lately. This does hurt, though. Can't he see? He can leave this place, he can leave it forever. With me. Far away from the memories, that fucking Cathedral, and from all of his skeletons.

"Because I'm fucked in the head, Nat. I am far past fixable. I'm a sick fuck, look what I have done to you. I thought it was okay," He runs his tattooed hands down his face and admits something that leaves me speechless in an instant. "You know what, I'll tell you why, Natalya. Did you know that just a few days ago, I'd decided in my mind I couldn't let you go. That I'd help you out of that Cathedral, but I knew I could never let you go. I had thoughts of bringing you to this very cabin and keeping you here for the rest of your life. You were going to be mine forever, and you had no say in the matter. So, while I'm thinking clearly, return to your Babushka tomorrow, and do not look back, Never speak with me again, Natayla. Ever. Because I don't want to stay away. As sick and selfish as that is. I am damn near eaten with infatuation. A dark obsession. I saw you as my pretty little doll. Moldable. Bendable. Beautiful. Perfect. My Dollface. I still do. That is why you must go alone without me."

For a moment, I'm at a loss for words at his admission, but then I do something that any sane person would think is worthy of grippy socks. I rush over, grab his face, and kiss him. Hard. Because fuck healthy choices, I just escaped a religious cult with a psycho Priest. If this is the last night I see Felix, after some serious horror movie shit, then I will make it count. If you're already walking through fire, you might as well dance. I'll just dance by therapizing out my assumed Stockholm Syndrome, before I go back to regular life tomorrow.

At first he stills, and I think he's going to pull away, but he doesn't. He cups my jaw with one of his hands, and gently slides to the tender column of my throat as he kisses me back with everything he has. Kissing Felix after all of the bullshit we've been through is world shatteringly electric. It feels like fire, ice, and it makes me question my sanity. All of which have my adrenaline pumping, and we break away to stare into each other's eyes. Neither of us say anything at first, but we don't have to. What our mouths don't say, our eyes do.

"Dollface,"Felix says under his breath between pants,"Is this my going away present?" He asks.

"It's whatever you want it to be, Doc. But I suppose it'll be a while until my next visit." My grin is sly, as wrap my arms around his waist.

"Hmm," He growls low, "then I better make this one last" he teases, his eyes lighting up mischievously.

"And how do you plan to do that?" I taunt, as I wrap my leg tightly around his hips, giving him gentle kisses between words.

The ice of his blue eyes darken, as he walks me through the living room to one of the doors in the hall, "I'm going to throw you to my bed, and feast on you like a savage fucking animal." His words cause me to shiver, and my cheeks flush hot.

And oh, does he keep that promise. I don't think Felix nor I relented. When one of us broke, and shattered, we would put each other back together again all night. Only to do it over again.

We'd only slept for three measly hours before my flight the next morning, and said our goodbyes.

I sit by the airplane window, watching over the people walking by on the pavement. My mind attempts to process the last few weeks of my life. It barely feels real, like a fever dream that's hardly in my mental grasp. Did I imagine it all? No, the scars on my back prove it. As does the bite mark Felix left on my thigh last night.

If I told anyone, would they believe me? Not likely. I'd probably get a free extended-stay vacation to Stables Mental Hospital. Complete with my very own gown and grippy cloth socks.

Just then the flight attendant brings me my drink and slips me a note. Lost in my thoughts, I mutter a thank you, as I lift the note open. My eyes go wide , and I glance up to scan the passengers around me, then I glance back down to the note. In beautiful writing it reads,

*Soon, Dollface.*

# CHAPTER 18

*Dollface*

Giving myself one last onceover in the mirror, I decide this is as good as it's going to get. They will hire me or they won't. Today I have a job interview at a new place I'd heard about through this new girl named Jasmine from my therapy group. It's an assistant position at a newer company called Trackers. It's a privately owned organization that investigates and tracks down cases of trafficking, abduction, or other crimes against women. Whether they be for religious cults, or other depraved reasons.

It's been six months since I returned home from Siberia. It's also been six months since I've heard from Felix. I don't know why, but I'd expected a call or text from him. Nothing. Radio silence. Which really strikes me as odd, considering his note. The note that's in my purse. The note that I'd kept like they were a promise, because in some twisted way I did want Felix in my life. After everything we'd been through, it feels like something is missing.

Except, for the past couple of weeks I've been getting this eerie feeling. Like somebody's watching me, everywhere I go. I keep telling myself that it is just the trauma, the paranoia-but I know better. It's my mind wishing he was here. Near me, even if he isn't.

I just need to see that he's okay, to know that he didn't stay in that place. A part of me still cares for him, even though I know it's not healthy.

◆ ◆ ◆

When I'm finally at the building of *Trackers*, the woman behind the front desk has her back to me when I first approach. After she turns around, I am stunned to see that it's Jasmine. She told me about the company, but I didn't know she worked here. Upon noticing me she smiles widely and walks me through a long hall, and into a spacious, new office. Her long, micro braids, twisted into the cutest space buns I've ever seen. Jasmine always has the cutest style. Like now, she's wearing a purple satin pants suit, with a matching top, and nude heels. Impeccable. I wish I could put myself together so easily. I glance down at my black turtleneck, and camel colored, suede skirt. It's cute, but if her wardrobe is the requirement, I may have to step it up.

"Here's the boss. You'll do great, Nat." She winks, and closes the door behind her. Then, the one she called *the boss* turns, and smirks down at me, with his piercing blue eyes staring right into mine. No way. It can't be-

"Felix." I whisper under my breath, and barely move a muscle. I'm too shell-shocked to do anything but stare at the man before me. It's like I'm seeing a ghost .

"I told you I'd be seeing you soon, Dollface. Did you miss me?" He taunts. Felix is so much more amused than I am.

"You run..Trackers?" I blink, my tone one of disbelief, as a heavy exhale escapes past my red-painted lips.

He leans back onto his desk, his palms flat against the ebony wood. His white, button down sleeves are rolled up to expertly showcase his tattoos. "Yes, I do." He answers, crossing his arms. "Surprised?" He asks.

"Yeah, actually? When? H-how?" I barely get out. Confused isn't even the word for it.

"I thought about what you said. About me needing to get away from there. I may have been conditioned and abused to believe Gurevich was right, but him wanting me to inflict those things onto you really broke me. It changed my perception, Natalya. After you left I went to a hospital. I got therapy, and I even got my brothers the help they needed. They didn't need much convincing to work for me, as I'd said before, Kai would do anything for Tati. The other two would do anything for me and Kai. So we left Siberia. Trained. We rebuilt our brains, our bodies. We are well built machines now. Now we only kill for the actual good. " He fills me in on recent events, gauging my reaction. "I missed you, Dollface. More than you know. I am so sorry it took me so long to get my shit together, but I wanted something to show for myself. Something to show you."

"What do you mean you only kill the bad guys at Trackers?" I question, my voice careful and even. If what he is saying is true, then Felix has come a long way, and a part of me hopes he is here to stay. A long way other than still committing crime, even if it is for the greater good.

"What I mean, Dollface, is here at Trackers we hunt religious cults and trafficking organizations around the world. Then, we take them out. We are pretty new, though. What I want to know is will you join me? I want you to work by my side, right along with me." The hope in his voice leaves a flutter deep in my chest, but he's asking me to make a commitment to turn the other way at murder. Is it so bad though, if he's saving people? There was a time when I would have taken a life in exchange for freedom, the thought makes me shutter. "What do you say, Dollface?"

"Yes. I will, but only if I get to make some of the decisions. I won't risk harming innocent people." I agree to join Trackers. If you're telling me I get to rid the earth of scum like Gurevich, then hell yes. Count me in. Just like that, all of my therapy went out the window.

At my agreement to work by his side, Felix's mouth slows into the biggest grin I've ever seen. "Good, you start tomorrow." He says, seeming more than pleased with my answer. "Just one more thing, Natalya." He demands, as I stand to walk away.

"Yes?" I ask, raising a brow at him. Is this the part where he tells me I'm a dumbass for believing his bullshit, redemption story? Maybe he will smuggle me onto a plane back to Siberia next.

"Go to dinner with me tonight. Eight p.m." He looks almost nervous, like he knows I'll tell him to go to hell. Which is what I should do, but I don't. Not after having him in front of me again. I can't, I won't.

"Okay, but don't be late." I agree, as I shut his office door behind me, and exit the building. I have a handsome date to get ready for. I wonder what my therapist would say about this. Oh well-what she doesn't know won't hurt her.

My phone pings as I'm swiping on a fresh coat of red lipstick, and I slip on my red v-cut dress. It's fitted to the body, with a deep v cut neckline, that has lace covering it to give the illusion of showing skin, but still leaving much to the imagination.

I glance down at my phone, and I am already fully aware of who it could be. A text from none other than Felix, telling me he is parked outside. My eyes roll and I grin before wiping it away. I can't let him see how eager I was to see him again. He has to know what he did was wrong, even if it brought him closer. In a trauma response, lusty kind of way anyway. No, as much as I tell myself that's all it is, I know it has to be more. Lust doesn't make you long for someone, for six months. With no contact. Nor does trauma, I think. Even if it is caused by being broken, I don't desire to be fixed.

Not because I enjoyed suffering, but because I am Felix Antonov's pretty, broken Dollface-and that is just how he likes me.

# EPILOGUE

# FELIX; ONE YEAR LATER

A year and a half has passed since Natayla and I escaped the horrific grasp of Father Gurevich's cleansing that had once tried to take hold of us. Our lives have transformed and changed significantly in these twelve months, since reuniting on our own terms, and running *Trackers*. Though scars and wounds of our experience in a religious cult are ingrained in us, we have grown stronger, closer, and more hungry for vengeance than ever.

The past year has been a clusterfuck of healing, determination, and most importantly- being consumed with each other. The tracking business I had built for us to run together —established in the shadows of our shared broken past—rapidly became successful. What had started as a small, mostly private company offering rapid tracking services has grown into so much more that I had imagined for us. We have a triumphant, discreet company, serving a variety of clients with dangerous and specific needs. All very important to us. My Dollface's attention to detail, combined with her bloodthirsty as hell commitment to offering freedom and the insurance of the brutal death of our client's assailants, has set *Trackers* apart from anything in existence. Clients trust us, knowing that Natayla's commitment to their well beings remains deeper than most.

Lucky for me, our business success is not my only triumph. There were many moments of vulnerability and mistrust, of course—especially in the beginning. There have been many nights when the burdens of our past experiences and memories would bubble to the surface. But in having each other, we were both able to heal. We have spent months in therapy and desired solace in each other. We knew not many would understand. Other than my brothers and Tati, who all work for our company. Natayla and I have found new ways to work through our afflictions, refusing to let the trauma ruin anything we have.

Every night I have spent with my beautiful Natalya has led up to this one. Something I thought I would maybe never get the opportunity to do after she got on that plane and left Siberia. Tonight I took her to the restaurant we had our first date as after she walked into my office a year ago, it is my Dollface's favorite place—a quiet, little seafood place right next to the beach, our little escape from the flashbacks of the Cathedral basement. A place where we forgot who we have been, and consume our obsessions of each other freely. It's here that I've decided to ask Natalya Lane to marry me.

"Natayla," I addressed her, dropping to one knee after we finished our meals, "we have lived through the craziest things together. We have seen every inch of one another's souls, bared and raw. Both the darkness and the light. There is nothing I have been more certain of in my entire life. You are already mine, but I want to officially spend the rest of my life with you, build a life, something we both need and deserve. Dollface, will you marry me?"

I don't know why I was so nervous, because without any uncertainty or pause, Natayla flashed me that gorgeous smile and said yes. Her full bottom lip quivering, and her pretty grey eyes filled with unshed tears. She has always been the most perfect thing I've ever seen. It isn't just the promise of marriage I'm offering her; it is my word that we will be continuing this life together—only bound by the chains we choose to set in place.

" Looks like I'm all yours. I love you, Felix." She grinned up at me, wrapping her arms around my neck.

"You were always mine, Dollface." I wink.

# BOOKS IN THIS SERIES

## *Tormented*

Dollface is book one in the Tormented series. There will be three novellas, that are all interconnected standalones.

## **Dollface**

Dollface is a horror novella, with dark romance themes. It is about a language exchange student named Natalya, who trusts the wrong friend.
After relocating across the globe, she is forced into a religious cult.

# DOLLFACE

www.ingramcontent.com/pod-product-compliance
Lightning Source LLC
Chambersburg PA
CBHW060332260626
47160CB00007B/2777